MAKE A SCENE

MIMI GRACE

CONTENT NOTES

These brief notes are for readers who need some insight into the contents of this novel. Some may view the following as spoilers.

- A pregnant supporting character
- A number of sexually explicit scenes

Chapter One

THERE WERE ONLY two things Retta Majors truly hated:
1. low-rise jeans 2. people who smugly corrected anyone
who misidentified Frankenstein as the monster. But today
she could add a third thing to her list.

"We're getting married!"

Retta stared unblinking at her cousin, Irene, and her
now fiancé, Chris, as they stood in the middle of the living
room with coordinated outfits and grins. At least, she
thought Chris was also smiling, but it was hard to tell with
the beard that reached his chest.

"In two months," Irene added, thrusting her left hand
in front of her to showcase the enormous rock on her
finger.

An eruption of joyous babble and congratulations
followed as family and friends converged on the couple.

Retta had only been at the gathering, pitched to her as
a casual birthday party for her Aunt Tina, for thirty
minutes before the announcement dropped.

While on the couch, sandwiched between two of the
oldest people in her family and with a Pomeranian on her

lap, Retta examined the feasibility of army-crawling out of the house.

"She's going to make such a beautiful bride," one of Retta's relatives said to no one in particular as she admired Irene in a pretty dress with bracelet-length sleeves.

"Can you believe it? Less than a year and he seals the deal," another said.

Retta placed the dog onto the carpet and unfolded her tall frame from the plastic-covered sofa, forcing a smile.

Where was Mrs. Whitfield with the wine?

The warmth sweeping through the room was evidence there were too many people packed into her aunt's modest sized house. She sidestepped the children in attendance who were taking advantage of the adults' excitement by performing an overly complicated dance. Retta managed to get to the adjoining kitchen without being stopped, but she found her aunt and uncle with a family friend chatting about the hot topic of the evening.

"What does he do?" the family friend who wore a headwrap and a bright purple lipstick asked.

They didn't notice her entrance, and Retta ignored them in turn for the open wine bottle nestled between abandoned plates and empty serving dishes on the counter. Now for the impossible task of finding a clean glass or cup in the cluttered kitchen.

"You know what? I don't know," her aunt replied. "Leroy, do you know?"

Her uncle stood with a glass half-filled with brown liquor, his slightly round stomach pressing against his dress shirt. His eyes remained glued to the living-room television playing the PGA Championship as he shook his head.

After (barely) rejecting a muffin pan as a viable drinking vessel, Retta said, "He's an engineer with a utility company."

She regretted her insertion into the conversation when the two women turned to her and oohed in unison.

"I remember when you girls were young and jumping rope in the driveway. Now look," the family friend said, gesturing toward Irene who'd applied every poise training she received as a pageant girl to hold court.

Retta nodded, retrieving a measuring cup from the drawer she'd opened.

Finally.

After several seconds her aunt said, "You must be so happy for her."

Retta looked at her over the brim of the cup. After swallowing a mouthful of wine and straightening her glasses, she said, "Mhmm. Very."

Actually, she felt like she'd woken up in a world where a hookah-smoking caterpillar existed, and she was trying not to freak-out.

Her aunt must've interpreted the edge in Retta's voice as longing because she said, "And of course, your time will come, baby."

The family friend nodded, threatening to undo her precariously knotted headwrap. "You need to try some of those dating apps. I've really come around to them since Janet—you know Janet—had success with the Bubbles one."

"Keep dating and trying because mighty oaks from little acorns grow," her aunt said.

Retta sighed and took another swing of wine before smiling big and saying, "Excuse me."

With brisk steps, she made her way to the restroom. And only once she was safely locked inside, did she drop her smile. While leaning against the door, Retta pulled out her phone and dialed the most frequently used number.

"Hey, this is Kym. Please consider leaving a text rather than a message after the beep."

"They're getting married," Retta said to the robot recording her. "I'm not bothered they're doing it. I'm annoyed I didn't see it coming." She hiccupped and picked at her chipping nail polish. "I don't know. I thought they'd eventually break up, and I wouldn't have to see his face at every family event. Also, who announces their engagement at someone else's—"

The click on the other end of the line told her she'd exceeded her recording limit, and before she could leave another message, a knock sounded at the door.

"One second," Retta said as she pressed her phone between her chin and chest while she washed her hands.

She exited the bathroom, and the reintroduction to the racket in the house made her stop short of the living room area. A dish of potpourri lay upturned on the floor from someone pushing the sofa into the side table, no doubt in an attempt to get closer to the golden couple.

Screw it.

Retta had carpooled with a family member, but she decided she'd grab her purse, say her goodbyes, and get an Uber home.

But during the second step of her escape plan, a shrill whistle drew everyone's attention back to the center of the living room.

Irene's father, a big man with broad shoulders and dark skin, whose voice and appearance were similar to Retta's own father's, joined the couple to say a few words.

Seeing no other option, Retta turned to listen.

"It took you two a while to get together, but your souls were meant for each other. Look" —he gestured between the three of them and the variations of blue they wore— "you're already dressing like part of the family."

A smattering of laughter followed.

Retta tempered down the impulse to roll her eyes at the concept of "soul mates". Irene and Chris had probably met at a function like this one, talking around a punch bowl about the music playing or maybe laughing at a joke the other said.

She'd once read most people end up with a partner who lives in walking or driving distance from them. That information made relationships less ethereal and more about proximity and convenience.

As the speech progressed, Retta felt the subtle looks people in the room gave her. She knew what they might be searching for: a slight twitch in her face, a stiff smile, or maybe pure, unmitigated misery.

Would this be how the wedding would unfold for Retta if she had a lapse in judgment and decided to attend? Everyone waiting for her to uncharacteristically collapse across a church pew or brood in shadowy corners of the reception hall like some soap opera villainess.

After the speech ended and a round of cheers was lifted, Retta made her move toward the front door. She found her nephew, niece, and two of her cousin's children playing with a balloon in the entryway.

Walking to the coat closet she asked, "What game are we playing?"

They all shrugged and continued to play, but her six-year-old niece, her brother's daughter, rushed up to her and wrapped her arms around Retta. "Do you think I can be a flower girl?"

"I don't know, mama. You'll have to ask Auntie Irene," Retta said as she tucked a few braids with beads on the end of them behind the child's ear.

"Are you going to the wedding?" her nephew asked as he stretched his body out to catch the falling balloon.

Retta hesitated. She didn't really need to be grilled by an eight-year-old on why she wouldn't be attending this particular celebration, so she said, "I like weddings. There's cake, dancing—"

"Mommy says you won't come," her niece said.

"Hm?"

"Yeah, she says you'd be too sad because you like Auntie Irene's boyfriend," her nephew added as he punted the balloon.

Retta tightly pressed her lips together. Obviously, the family news cycle had been slow, because she thought she'd stopped being the topic of gossip months ago. Maybe she could convince her cousin to get another face tattoo.

Poor Retta. Such a shame what happened.

The sentiment haunted her.

"I thought you were leaving?" her nephew asked as she chucked her coat back into the closet.

"Nope," Retta said. "I've changed my mind. The party just started."

———

Retta was acutely attuned to certain sounds. In eighth grade, it was the scrape of the cafeteria chairs positioned exactly five tables down signaling her crush had left his seat. When she worked at a call center after high school, it was the short exhale a potential donor would release before they either hung up or cussed her out. And these days it was the tinkering, however minuscule, in her bakery.

The specificity and joys of working at Dutch Oven Bakeshop—the tranquility of early mornings and the smell of various doughs—had been diminished, however, by the stop-start rattling of their water heater. Considering how late she'd gotten home last night, the noise felt like a personal attack.

"We can't work in these conditions," one of her bakers, Philippa, said from her place near the ovens where she was scoring sourdough with a sharp blade.

Retta threw a little flour on her work surface. "It's temporary."

Omar, a pastry chef and the only man who worked at the bakery, snorted.

She'd been saying that for weeks since contacting her evasive landlord about the problem. It was now clear the refrain helped her from losing her mind more than it comforted her team.

"I'm sorry. I know, I'm late." Cheyenne, their spring intern, burst through the swinging kitchen doors then. Her long braids and apron strings flying behind her. "I had to park two blocks away."

"That's another problem," Omar said, pointing at Cheyenne. "What are we doing about the parking?"

"Yes," Philippa said, crossing her heavily tattooed arms. "Is that temporary too?"

Retta sighed. The parking lot dedicated to the staff of businesses in the strip mall was where hierarchies were forged. Older businesses in the complex had premium spaces, while newer stores were left with the least desirable spots.

Dutch Oven had paid their dues for over a year, parking in a cramped area near a huge green garbage bin dubbed The Hulk. But when the spa next door had moved out, her bakeshop secured three roomy parking spaces. Well, at least they thought they had until Spotlight Boxing Studio started moving in next door three months ago.

Retta looked at her staff. "I've been leaving Post-it notes on their windshields."

"Okay, but it's obviously not working," Philippa said over the clanking water heater.

A headache pressed aggressively against Retta's temples. She briefly wondered if she'd find relief if she loosened the low bun she'd smoothed down with Eco-Styler gel and a prayer. "When I have a moment, I'll go over there and make an official request for them to stop parking in our spaces."

Eight times out of ten, she and her staff got their rightful spots because they were at the bakery before dawn, but she wanted to guarantee that would always be the case.

That comment appeased her staff, and they returned to their prep work until they opened Dutch's doors at seven AM. The first few hours saw regulars picking up their pastries and tarts on their way to work.

"Smells fantastic as usual," Tamara, a receptionist at a realtor office nearby, said.

"Thank you," Retta replied, letting the compliment seep into her soul. "Also, you'll be happy to know we're bringing back the lavender lemonade in a few weeks."

The woman waved her hand in celebration before finishing off her transaction.

By midmorning, Retta had completed some admin work and made sure the glass cases were streak free.

Her best friend, Kym, found her at the front when she walked into the bakery, mindlessly rubbing her very pregnant belly.

Retta relieved her friend of her bag. "Okay, dress." She gestured to her friend's light pink outfit that complemented the lilac walls surrounding them.

"Thank you, but, *girl*," Kym said.

The heft of the word let Retta know her friend had things to say, and nothing would distract her.

"Let me grab something," Kym said, retrieving her wallet and walking over to the front counter.

Kym was one of the few people in her life who insisted on paying for everything she ate in the bakery.

She returned with food and plopped down in her seat. Her curly hair bounced about before settling around her plump face. "All right, so this crisis—"

"I wouldn't call it a crisis per se," Retta said.

"You left me a two-minute voicemail."

"Yes, but I've had time to process it, and I'm fine now."

Kym studied her. "Okay, say that again, but this time make me believe it."

"I was caught off guard."

"But other than that, you're fine?"

"Yeah." Retta ran her fingers over the swirls that made up the white marble table. "Their e-invitation arrived in my inbox this morning—"

Kym snapped her fingers. "Uh-uh. No. No. Don't do that. Delete the e-invite and mute them on social media for the year. The wedding and honeymoon will come and go, and you won't have to see a picture or hear a conversation about it."

"Well…"

Her friend froze with a croissant halfway to her mouth. "You're not going to the wedding, right?"

She scrunched her round nose.

"Retta."

"She's family."

"Retta!"

"I have to."

Her friend made a sound between a sigh and a groan. "You *have* to eat. You *have* to drink water. You *have* to compliment me on my outfit every time you see me but"— she leaned in as much as her belly would allow and lowered her voice—"you don't have to go to your cousin's wedding. Especially when she's marrying your ex-boyfriend."

When she spelled out her situation, the right choice seemed obvious.

"The thing is, I don't want to seem bothered," Retta said.

"You left me a two-minute voicemail," her friend repeated.

"As I said, I was in shock."

"Okay, fine. But listen, the way he dumped you and moved on so quickly? No one would blame you for not showing up. You can't tell me attending that wedding will be the best use of your time."

Retta leaned back in her seat. "You want the truth?"

"Always," her friend replied.

"This wedding is my chance to finally show my family, show him, I'm not wilting or defeated."

With a breakup and career setback happening around the same time, Retta couldn't be around her family, even a year later, without receiving a concerned hand on her shoulder or generic encouragement.

And it wasn't for a lack of trying to appear jovial. She'd muted her feelings from the start. The last thing she'd wanted to do was give everyone access to her hurt, her vulnerability. Only a few people in her life knew how shaken she'd been by the back-to-back disappointments. And she intended to keep it that way.

Her friend studied her. "So, you're going to the wedding?"

"I'm going to the wedding."

"Fine," Kym said, with a loud clap. "I'll book time off."

"It's out of town, and the timing won't work," Retta said, looking at her friend's stomach.

"Yeah, I guess slipping on my own amniotic fluid wouldn't look great in pictures. Solo then?"

"Absolutely not. I need a date."

It was a conclusion Retta had come to before passing out for the night. Showing up to her ex's wedding alone seemed like it would be as enjoyable as stubbing her toe on the corner of her bed. And what said, "I'm not pressed; I've moved on" like a new boyfriend? It didn't matter if she had because perception wasn't held back by the truth.

"Oh?" Kym asked.

"Yeah, why not?"

Kym pursed her lips and nodded. "If you need me to set you up, I know someone you might like."

"So, you've been holding out on me?" Retta asked, squinting.

"You know good and damn well whenever I bring up dating, you talk about your busy schedule and your working vibrator," Kym said, mouthing the last word.

"Ok, well," Retta said, adjusting her glasses. "I've been thinking for weeks about how I should get back out there, you know? And this is the little nudge I need."

"Of course."

Retta nodded and smirked before saying, "And you'll be proud to know despite my ridiculous schedule and working vibrator, I've taken the initiative and already have a date lined up."

Chapter Two

IT WAS the end of a long day, and Retta stood in the parking lot with her team members on either side of her, studying the large truck boxing in her car. She was being screwed over, even though she got her desired spot.

"Are they trying to intimidate us into giving up?" Omar asked.

"That's not happening," Retta said, turning around. "Have a good evening. I'll see you all tomorrow."

Walking toward the front of the building, Retta quickened her pace. She had a small window to drive home, get ready, and meet her date at the bistro.

The gym's glass door opened easily, and she was met with red and black walls that had replaced the mint green of the spa that once operated there. The smell of paint still clung to the air. The front desk was unattended, and Retta stared hard at the place where a service bell should've been.

Natural instinct told her to wait there and hope someone came along to help her, but time was slipping.

Walking around the transformed room, she peeked around the corner to find an empty corridor.

"Hello?" she said.

The city's unofficial fifth season of road construction would make traffic delays inevitable.

"Hello," she said louder.

Walking down the hallway, Retta arrived at a landing where changing rooms lined the wall to her left and a staircase led to what she could see from her spot was a square gym.

The sound of someone hitting a bag reverberated through the space. It was accompanied by sharp hissing and grunting noises.

A needling awkwardness in her stomach formed, and the drop in the initial spike of adrenaline left her feeling out of place. But she straightened her shoulders against the impulse to flee and took a couple of steps down the stairs toward the sound. However, she only made it halfway before she caught sight of a shirtless man turned away from her, punching a bag with strong fists.

The muscles in the man's back swelled with each move. His dark brown skin all but reflected the bright lights hanging above him, and the sweat looked like it had been strategically placed with a spray bottle.

There had to be someone wearing more clothes who could help her.

As Retta retraced her steps, the man stopped punching the bag. She automatically flattened herself against the wall on the other side of the staircase, narrowly avoiding tumbling to her death. The massive headphones he wore would prevent him from hearing her, but she still held her breath.

Maybe she would've been better off screaming at the top of her lungs in the front entrance because she was about to get busted. But the man resumed his activity seconds after the amusing thought of being barred from a gym, of all places, crossed Retta's mind.

Straightening, she turned to finally leave, but her path was obstructed by a stocky guy with red hair. His shirt had the gym's logo on the front of it.

He frowned. "Can I help you?"

"I'm sorry," she whispered.

She met him at the top of the staircase. "I'm Retta," she said, continuing to whisper. "I own the bakery next door—"

"You own the what?" he asked loudly.

Retta winced. Pushing down her embarrassment, she repeated her introduction at a normal volume. "I think one of your vehicles is blocking my car."

"Oh, my bad."

They walked out of the building together, and he moved the large truck out of the way.

"Thank you," Retta said, as the man hopped out of the vehicle.

He gave her a nod and walked away.

"Oh, and welcome to the neighborhood."

He barely stopped to acknowledge her statement.

"And just so you know, these three spots," she pointed to the ones she referenced, "are assigned to me and my staff."

He shrugged. "You'll have to talk to Duncan or Anthony about that."

"And they are?"

"The owners," the young man said.

"Right. Well, thanks again."

———

All the rushing ended up being for nothing because Retta arrived well before her date. When he eventually showed, she spent ninety minutes enduring his bad table manners and long-winded explanations about his business that sounded very much like an MLM.

It was, therefore, no surprise when, days later, she was parked in front of a coffee shop applying lip gloss before a date Kym had set up for her.

She took deep breaths and shook out her hands. There was something about not knowing what her date looked like that had her overthinking things. Would she be attracted to him? What if he didn't eat gluten? Did her glasses magnify her wonky winged eyeliner?

Grabbing her purse and the latest issue of *Dream Big* magazine from the passenger seat, Retta exited her car.

The hissing and whirring of the barista coffee machines greeted her upon entering the shop. She pushed up her glasses on her nose and looked for a vacant table amongst the college-aged patrons. She was early, so when she spotted her date, Steve, her stomach did a little somersault.

He faced away from the entrance and wore the preplanned red jacket and had an identical copy of the magazine in her hand on the small round table in front of him.

She quickly joined the line at the front counter to order herself a drink, and when she turned around, she half-expected to find Steve no longer there. But he was, and she pushed her shoulders back and maneuvered through a sea of white, minimalist furniture to get to him.

Clearing her dry throat, she said, "Hey." Her hand rose in a brief wave that didn't go above her waist.

The man looked up from his phone, and the ice-breaking joke Retta had planned to say, vanished from her mind.

Up until this moment, she'd sooner believe in time travel and theories on Tupac's presence in Cuba, than the idea she'd ever be on a date with someone this attractive.

This man, with a jawline and cheekbones that threatened to pierce the russet-colored skin lying over it, was the most beautiful person she'd ever seen in real life.

One of his thick eyebrows raised. "Hi?"

Right, he didn't know what she looked like either.

"Retta," she said, lifting her copy of the business magazine. She laughed and quickly slid into the seat opposite of him, piling her purse and jacket on the empty third seat.

"It's great to finally meet you. Kym's told me so much about you."

Steve frowned slightly.

"Not *so* much, just enough," she quickly added, laughing again. This time it had a tinny quality she didn't recognize. She ran her suddenly clammy palms down the front of her skirt and stockings.

Speak.

"So, Steve, you're an accountant," she said as she moved to place her chin on her fist, accidentally stabbing herself with the ring she wore. "How do you like it?" she asked, rubbing the sore spot.

He opened his mouth to say something, but the barista shouted into the shop, "One medium iced dolce latte."

"That's mine," Retta said a little too loudly as she got up to retrieve her drink. Okay, she needed to get it together. Enough of the boring questions and jittery behavior. She'd hate for him to have the upper hand by knowing she was thrown by his appearance. Besides, she was a woman with a lot to be proud of: she was a business owner, someone who flossed daily, and she once used a meditation app for fourteen days straight.

When she returned to their table, she found Steve smiling, revealing a dimple in his left cheek. She studied it.

"My name's not Steve," he said once she was seated.

Retta pulled her eyes from the offending cheek to look at the man in his eyes. "Pardon?"

"I don't know who Steve is, but it's not me."

Oh, no. She'd mixed up his name with someone else's. Like that time she'd called the mailperson at her apartment by her mechanic's name for several weeks before the poor woman delivering packages corrected her. In Retta's defense, their names were incredibly similar.

Retta dramatically grimaced. "I'm sorry, I have so many people's names swimming in my head. Remind me of yours."

Not-Steve studied her before chuckling. "I'm gonna guess you're here for a date." He leaned in. "I'm not your date."

Several horrifying seconds passed. "Oh my God," she whispered. Her face stung as if she'd been slapped. This was definitely worse than mixing up names. "This is," Retta said, picking up her purse and jacket. "Embarrassing." She scooted out of her seat to stand. "I should've—"

"Don't worry about it," the complete stranger said, smiling again.

She wanted to be swaddled in the heat of the earth's core at that moment.

"Seriously," he added.

Retta could barely look at him. The universe must've smelled her desperation for a date.

"Is that him?" Not-Steve asked, nodding toward someone over her left shoulder.

She turned to see a white man, wearing a red jacket,

sitting a few tables away with a copy of *Dream Big* magazine propped up on fake flowers at the center of the table.

Retta slowly closed her eyes as she turned back to face
the man she'd ambushed. "Probably."

He looked down at his own clothes. "Understandable
mistake. We're practically twins."

She was supposed to laugh, but all she could manage
was, "I'm gonna go now."

"Have fun," he said.

This afternoon could be salvaged.

"Steve?" Retta said as she arrived at her actual date's
table. She ignored the urge to ask him for a
government-issued ID.

"Retta?" he asked, standing up to give her a hug once
she nodded. "You look amazing."

"Thank you," she said as they both took their seats.

"I've been so nervous about this date."

His admittance pulled her to the present. Her shoulders dropped and she smiled at him. "Same."

"Yeah?"

They both laughed.

Retta's laugh morphed into a choking cough when she
noticed Not-Steve approaching their table with her
forgotten iced beverage.

Without a word, Not-Steve smiled and handed her the
drink.

She thought she said thank you, but wasn't quite sure.

Actual-Steve briefly turned to look behind him. "What
was that about?"

"I left my drink on his table. No big deal. Anyway, so
you're an accountant?"

Chapter Three

RETTA WAS STARING off into the distance when Philippa waved her hand in front of her. "You okay?"

Retta shook herself out of the stupor and looked up. "Yeah, I'm fine."

Philippa raised her eyebrows. "You sure? You seem out of it today."

That was true, and it was the byproduct of falling asleep late after reading fluff pieces about getting left on read. She'd thought she'd hit it off with Steve, but he hadn't responded to her texts in three days.

One would think after being dumped for her younger cousin, Retta would have built some sort of thick skin, but to her horror, Steve's passive rejection stung.

"I'm sure," Retta said to Philippa, giving her an appreciative smile.

As they got into the bulk of the work, they remained quiet letting the pop music playing from an old radio on a bench at the back of the kitchen lull them into a rhythm.

"Oh," Philippa said after some time. "Did I tell you

guys that I met one of the trainers from next door yesterday?"

Omar stopped rolling the croissant dough and looked up. "No. Tell."

Retta similarly turned to Philippa. She'd sent a welcome basket over to the gym this morning in hopes it would ingratiate her with the owners when she finally asked them to stop parking in her spots.

"All I'm saying is if I wasn't so busy to date, I'd be all over him."

"Yeah, nothing hurts dating or a booty call like having a nine p.m. bedtime," Omar said. "Maybe Retta can tell us how she does it."

Retta jerked her head back. "What's that supposed to mean?"

"Oh, please. Like we haven't noticed you rushing off every other day after work," Philippa said.

"Or coming in with a change of clothes," Omar said.

"The extra makeup."

Retta looked between her staff members and said, "Wow, I work with the Feds."

Cheyenne popped her head in the kitchen. "Hey, Retta?" the young woman whisper-shouted.

"What's up?"

"Someone's here to see you."

She looked up. "Who?"

"Crap, I didn't ask," Cheyenne said, biting her lip. "Give me a second."

"No, it's fine," Retta said, wiping her hands on a towel and removing her apron.

It was probably Lincoln, the liaison for one of her ingredient distributors. He said he might be dropping in sometime today. "I'll be right out."

Entering the front area of the bakery, she did a quick

scan for the familiar face but came up short. Turning to Cheyenne who stood behind the counter, Retta frowned and shrugged.

Her intern responded by pointing to a Black man at the condiment station near the door. The man had closely cut hair with clean lines and an incredibly wide back that had her drawing nearer.

After securing a lid onto a disposable coffee cup, the man turned around, and it was a wonder Retta's jaw didn't come off its hinges when her mouth dropped.

Not-Steve, the man she'd mistaken as her coffee date, stood in front of her with his cup positioned for a drink.

How in a city of more than two million people, did she run into the one person she'd thoroughly embarrassed herself in front of? She'd think he'd tracked her down if his face didn't mirror the shock she felt.

Slowly, however, his wide lips turned upward, and goosebumps formed on her arms at the emergence of his dimple. What was he doing here?

She forced herself not to shrink as he closed the distance between them. When she'd first seen him at the cafe, she hadn't appreciated how built and tall he was. Naturally, the visual of him hoisting her over his shoulder came unencumbered.

"Hi, I'm Duncan," the man said, taking a drink from his cup. "I own the gym next door."

———

Duncan Gilmore watched the woman he met last week, blink several times behind glasses that sat firmly on her round nose.

In the coffee shop, she'd appeared and left as suddenly as a gust of wind. But standing in front of her now,

Duncan had time to take in the soft details of her face that were accentuated because her hair was pulled back in a bun.

"Retta," she said, schooling her features and sticking out her hand for him to shake.

He accepted it, taking note of the dusting of flour against her brown skin. Of course he remembered her. How could he not? He was also positive she recognized him too.

"Welcome to the neighborhood," she said.

"Are we pretending like we've never met?" he whispered, liking the way her eyes widened slightly.

She shook her head. "That would be silly... unless you'd like to be my fifth favorite person."

Duncan smiled, leaning his shoulder against the column beside him. "Don't tell me you're still embarrassed about the mix-up."

The various gold earrings in her ear caught the light as she ducked her head. "Not one of my finest moments."

"Okay, we can forget it. Let's try this again," Duncan said, straightening his posture. "It's nice to meet you, Retta... for the very first time in my entire life."

She snorted. "Welcome to the neighborhood."

Despite having agreed seconds ago to forget their first meeting, Duncan was curious about how her real date had ultimately ended. He'd left fifteen minutes after their interaction with a fleeting wish that it hadn't been a mistake.

"Well, I don't want to mess with your day or nothing. I only dropped in to say hi," Duncan said after shaking himself internally. This particular edition of introducing himself to the business owners in the complex had to end before he started asking the pretty baker invasive questions.

"Oh, actually, while you're here, I should discuss something with you," she said, stepping closer to him.

"You're new around here, so you wouldn't know how things operate yet, but each business has their own parking spots. My staff and I have the three to the far left."

Duncan frowned. "There was nothing about assigned parking in the rental agreement."

"W-well, it's more of an unofficial thing that we all follow," she said.

"And let me guess, my gym gets the spaces nobody wants."

Retta shoved her hands into the pockets of her overalls. "Yes."

Several seconds of silence passed before something clicked. "You're the one who's been leaving the threatening Post-its on our cars."

"Uh, yeah. They weren't supposed to come off that way," she said, squirming in place. "You really lose tone in writing."

For weeks he and the staff had been finding notes that demanded they move. They hadn't known who they were from, so they ignored them.

"I'll have to discuss it with my business partner and get back to you," Duncan said, already knowing it was going to be a battle. They weren't going to give up the spots. "Do you have a card or something?"

"Yeah, give me a second," Retta replied.

As she reached over the counter, his eyes traveled up the length of her long legs. They seemed to go on forever, but they progressed into the curve of her butt where two faint flour handprints sat on either cheek.

"Here you go," she said, turning back around and handing him the card.

Clearing his throat, he studied the information.

"No pressure."

"All right, great," he said, heading toward the door. "Thanks."

"*Donut* be a stranger," she called out.

Duncan looked back in time to catch her wince.

"I'll forget that one too," he said.

"Fourth favorite person," she replied.

He left the bakery with a smile, and within a few seconds, he entered his gym, Spotlight Boxing Studio. It was a little surreal to know that this was his reality. From the red walls to their logo etched on the glass door, everything had fallen into place for him and his partner. Except maybe how they were now battling for parking space.

Jessie, one of the trainers, was working the front desk between her classes and gave him a nod in greeting.

"Hey, how's it going?" Duncan asked, approaching the counter.

"Good," Jessie said, taking a bite from a shortbread cookie. "Busy."

He gestured to her hand. "Where did you get that from?"

Food, especially sweets and dessert, didn't last long at Spotlight despite Duncan's best efforts to keep the fridge stocked up for his team.

"Oh, from this," Jessie said, leaning back in her chair and retrieving a large basket with an extravagant purple bow. "Someone from the bakery next door delivered it this morning."

Unfolding the cloth that hid the contents of the gift basket, he studied the remaining pastries. He wondered if Retta had handpicked them herself. When he took a bite out of the most appealing one, the noise around him disappeared. All he could concentrate on was the tartness of the raspberries on the pastry. The way the tip of his tongue zinged before the slightly sweet custard that accompanied the dessert mellowed out the flavor.

"Good, right?" Jessie asked.

He nodded, choosing two more pastries to try.

Chatter filled the foyer as the one o'clock drill-based class was let out. Duncan smiled at all the sweaty, giddy faces emerging from one of the downstairs gyms.

"Have a good afternoon," he told several of them.

His best friend and business partner, Anthony, followed behind the hoard of people, equally as sweaty as his students but with his typical scowl in place.

He met Anthony at the water fountain where he was filling up his bottle. The big guy was someone who at first glance seemed intimidating. Well, also at second glance. Truthfully, even when you got to know him, he wasn't exactly a ray of sunshine. But he was always kind and was a hit with literally anyone who took his classes.

"How did networking go?" Anthony asked, pushing his curly hair from his eyes.

"Fine. Except we're apparently infringing on some unspoken parking rules."

Throwing the towel over his shoulder, his friend asked, "What do you mean?"

"There's assigned parking," Duncan said.

A big reason they picked this location for the gym was for those spaces.

His business partner rubbed his face roughly with his hands. "There was nothing about that on the rental agreement."

"I know, but we're trying to play nice and not make enemies," Duncan said, taking a bite from his croissant. If the persistence of the Post-it notes were any indication, Retta would take it personally if they didn't come to some sort of understanding.

Anthony, however, was similarly stubborn. "No way. It's not happening. If we're not legally obliged, who cares about angry neighbors?"

Duncan let out a sigh. "We'll discuss it and come up with a compromise when you're less…"

"Less what?"

"Grumpy. Less grumpy," Duncan said, patting his friend on the back. "Please eat something."

In one swift motion, Anthony grabbed the pastries still in Duncan's hand and placed them in his mouth.

"I meant literally anything else."

———

During his last class of the day, Duncan wiped the sweat from his brow with the side of his forearm before speaking into the headset, "Hook your right arm above your head. Stretch those triceps. They worked hard today."

He looked out into his students' faces, obscured by the dim lights in the studio.

As the upbeat music transitioned to chill, vibey hip hop, he said, "All right, one more deep inhale."

The class mimicked the way he swung his arms above his head. "Now exhale. Thank you all for joining me tonight. Hope you enjoyed yourself."

People scattered to the edge of the studio to collect their belongings.

"And if you all could grab a disinfectant towel and wipe down your punching bag, that would be great," he said.

As he cleaned his own equipment, a woman in her thirties approached him. "I was nervous about coming. I thought it would be too intense for me, but I loved it."

"That's great, thank you. Hope to see you again," he said.

Walking over to the exit, he gave each person who left the gym area a goodbye and a smile. And before long it was only him and his older sister, Gwen.

She leaned on the floor to ceiling mirror at the front of the class.

"What did you think?" he asked, walking to her.

"Meh."

He raised his eyebrows.

She threw her towel at him. "You know it was great."

He grinned at her. They were two years apart and had always been close. Being the older sibling, however, had made her a little bossy growing up. But she'd also taken her job as firstborn seriously and had been the best role model. Maybe that's what made her such a great school teacher now.

"You came in late," he said.

"I was at the school and lost track of time." She watched him tidy the gym. "Do you need help?"

He tossed a bottle of glass cleaner at her. "You can get your fingerprints off my mirror."

As she sprayed and wiped down areas of the glass, Gwen said, "You've been ignoring my texts."

"Not the important ones," Duncan replied.

"All of them are important," his sister said, flipping the end of one of two large cornrows over her shoulder.

"Debatable."

"So, are you coming to brunch?" Gwen asked.

Duncan let out a heavy sigh. "Maybe."

His sister turned to him. "You can't make me go on my own again."

Sunday Brunch was a monthly Gilmore family tradition and obligation after some family therapist recommended it almost a decade ago.

The hectic months leading up to Spotlight's grand opening had given him an excuse to miss the gatherings. He could probably get away with skipping another one, but he felt bad he'd left his sister to deal with their parents alone.

Closing his eyes, he said, "I'll be there."

"Great," she said, returning to mirror cleaning. "Oh, and if you're bringing whoever you're dating this month, please make sure she's not like the last one."

"I told you I didn't know Kennedy was going to do all that," Duncan said, cringing at the memory of the woman's conspiracy theory tirade. "But I'm also not seeing anyone at the moment."

Gwen squinted. "Really?"

"Yeah. This," he gestured around him, "has been taking up my time for months."

"The women of the city will understand."

Duncan made a mocking laugh.

"But on a serious note"—Gwen looked around —"Time well spent. And Mom and Dad can't stop bragging."

"I'm sure you'll get some award soon and oust me as their favorite child."

"Oh, I know," she said. "I'm throwing you a bone in the meantime."

Chapter Four

DURING THE LAST hour of the workday, Retta looked up from her conversation with Cheyenne to see Irene's mother, Wendy, enter the bakeshop. It was such an unexpected appearance that Retta stopped talking mid-sentence.

Her aunt looked like she was fresh out of the salon chair with her perfectly pressed bob that swished from side to side as she approached the front counter.

"Wow, I haven't been here since your grand opening," Aunt Wendy said, looking around the store.

They made eye contact, and it was as if they simultaneously remembered how at that time Retta was still dating Chris. He'd stood by her side as she made a toast to business longevity. Now he was going to be her son-in-law.

Retta neatly placed her hands on the counter in front of her. "A lot of trial and error, but I like it now."

"It's beautiful," her aunt replied quickly.

"Are you looking for something specific today?" Retta asked.

"Oh, right," the older woman said, gently smacking

her temple. "Chris and Irene are having an engagement party of sorts that'll also work as her bridal shower, and I wanted to know if I can order one of those macaron towers you sell."

Cheyenne, like the impassioned intern she was, appeared with an order form on an iPad. Luckily, this type of order had a quick turn around, so they usually could fulfill even the most last-minute requests.

Retta's aunt filled out the form but momentarily looked up to ask, "Are you coming to the party?"

Seeing as Retta still didn't have a suitable date, her impulse for the last week had been to text her cousin and cancel her RSVP to the wedding. But whenever that urge surfaced, she remembered the humiliation that surrounded her breakup. She couldn't yield.

Internally shaking herself out of her head, Retta looked at her Aunt Wendy and said, "Yeah, I'll be there."

The older woman smiled before ducking her head to finish her request. "I also saw you'd RSVPed a plus one to the wedding."

Of course this was the time her aunt wanted to go over this particular detail.

"I did."

"Is it a special someone?" her aunt asked, and to perhaps eliminate any confusion with what she might mean by "special someone," she accompanied her question with a wink.

There were a couple of customers still in her shop, and her team was in earshot. "Hey, Auntie, why don't you text me. You have my number, right?"

Her aunt squinted. "Okay," she said almost pensively. "But remember catering is paid by the person. We lose if someone who said they were coming doesn't show up."

Retta smiled and nodded. Way to apply pressure on her date that very evening.

After Cheyenne completed the transaction, Aunt Wendy left the store with an order confirmation form and a box of madeleines.

Upon closing up shop for the day, Retta got ready for her date in the small bathroom.

When she emerged, she was met with sincere compliments from Omar and Philippa.

"Who's it today?" Omar asked as they walked together to their vehicles.

"A graphic designer," Retta said. Or was he the college admission's officer? The profiles were starting to run together.

Drawing nearer to her car parked on the street, she was pleased to see no ticket flapping underneath her windshield wiper today. While her staff helped her load in some baskets of laundry into her back seat, she spotted Duncan hauling two garbage bags.

"Who's that?" Omar asked.

"One of the owners of the gym," Retta said as they all watched Duncan dump the trash into the green bin.

"When's this parking mess getting resolved?" Philippa asked.

It had been two days since she'd brought it up to Duncan. "Hopefully soon."

She was giving him a few more days, but Retta was tired of playing "has my car been towed or did I forget where I parked it".

Duncan must've felt the intensity of several pairs of eyes searing into the back of his head because he suddenly looked over in their direction. All three of them struggled to find a natural orientation that didn't look like they'd been staring at him for the last twenty seconds.

"This is awkward," Philippa said.

Retta braved a look and caught Duncan waving.

She returned the greeting, and he started jogging toward them.

"I-is he coming this way?" Omar asked, squinting.

"Yes," Retta said. "Don't be weird."

"Never," Philippa said, before placing one palm awkwardly on the side of Retta's car and the other on her hip like a bad pin-up model.

"Jesus," Retta said under her breath.

"I didn't get a chance to thank you for the gift basket," Duncan said when he arrived in front of them. "It didn't last long."

"I'm glad you enjoyed it," Retta said.

He introduced himself to her team. In the process, he complimented Philippa on her tattoos and asked Omar about the backpack he wore.

"What was your favorite thing you tried?" Omar asked.

"Oh, hands down the blueberry scone with the…"

"The lemon glaze," Retta said.

"Yeah," Duncan said before closing his eyes and producing an exaggerated shiver. "Flaky and buttery. There'd be a problem if I could make them myself. Do you have a recipe?"

"I'd need your firstborn child and hair follicles as payment," Retta said.

"Done," he replied without skipping a beat.

She laughed, and he opened his mouth to say something, but someone called for him from the back entrance of the gym.

"I'll catch you later," Duncan said.

Once he was out of earshot, Philippa said, "I might get my ass a boxing gym membership."

Retta bid the two of them a good evening and entered her car. She had a date to get to.

Before she could pull out into the street, however, a message came through her phone. She laughed when she read the text her would-be date sent: **Hey, so sorry this is last minute, but raincheck?**

Chapter Five

AS DUNCAN STEPPED into the house he grew up in, a knot formed in the pit of his stomach. He wasn't holding his breath that it would fade at any point during brunch today.

"Hi," he said as he entered the bright yellow kitchen. He found his mom in front of the well-used stove and kissed her on the cheek before washing his hands.

"You made it," his mother said, beaming at him as she placed her hands on her hips.

Gwen laughed from her place at the dining table. She was occupied with marking students' work, so she didn't catch his cutting look.

"What do you want me to do?" Duncan asked.

She handed him a plate of pancakes and a jug of orange juice.

"How're the first weeks going at the gym?" his mother asked as she continued to flutter about in the kitchen.

"Good," Duncan said, placing the food on the table. "We got a nice feature in a business magazine. Also, we're seeing decent monthly and annual pass purchases."

"Look at my baby," his mother said as she joined them at the table.

His sister put her work away, and they studied the meal spread out in front of them.

"It's a shame the food is growing cold," his mother said after a moment, still smiling. She looked at the time on the stove before turning back to face her children. "Just like your father to be late for something scheduled."

But it was as if speaking about Malcolm Gilmore's tardiness made him miraculously appear.

"Hello, hello, hello," Duncan's dad said, his voice ringing through the house. When he entered the dining area, he slapped Duncan's back and gave Gwen's shoulders a squeeze.

He looked over to their mom and said, "Trudy."

"Malcolm," she replied, fluffing the short curls on her head.

The greeting was on par with how they interacted nowadays. Before, there might have been a peck on the cheek or a cold hug. If nothing else, Duncan appreciated the lack of pretense. It had been six months since his parents separated. His father moved out soon after the announcement; however, you wouldn't be able to tell by looking at the place. Plants his father had nurtured for years were still in the house. The bookshelf remained packed with his books. Even the coat closet still smelled like his cologne.

They all settled around the table and filled their plates. A breeze filtered in through the open sliding door, carrying with it the laughter of the neighborhood children.

"Where's Eric?" their dad asked Gwen.

"He's on a business trip," his sister said of her long-term boyfriend.

"One day we'll have everyone at the table," their mom said, laughing lightly.

For a while, they ate in silence.

"A bit cold," his father said after a forkful of pancakes.

Their mother took a sip from her glass and said, "Well, if you'd shown up a little earlier maybe—"

"Mom, I think he means the wind," Gwen said, standing up to close the sliding door to the small backyard.

"Oh," their mother said. "Sorry."

"That's okay, Trudy."

Duncan looked between his parents. This separation was doing wonders for their communication.

"I know it's hard for you to turn off the nagging after thirty-two years," he continued.

Cutlery clanged as Duncan and his sister simultaneously let them fall against their plates.

Their mother laughed humorlessly. "And as always I wouldn't have to nag if you regularly did the right thing."

"Well, I'm sorry I can't give you perfection."

"I never wanted perfection. Just effort," his mother said.

There was a beat of silence where his parents stared at each other. The calm before the storm, if you will. When the outright bickering commenced, Duncan sighed and sat back in his seat.

The chosen topic for this particular argument was anything remotely annoying the other person did in the past three decades. They didn't seem deterred by the fact they literally didn't have to do this anymore. They were separated. Soon to be divorced. Were they not tired?

There'd been periods of relative harmony in their marriage, but it wouldn't last more than three months. As a kid, Duncan had tried to prolong that time of peace by exaggerating events that had happened at school. His sister, on the other hand, chose to appeal to their teacher parents by presenting good grades and even better behavior.

Having company over also helped reduce the likelihood of a fight. But as soon as he got his driver's license and a crappy car, he didn't have to dread the end of the three month peace period because he could simply leave when things got loud.

Duncan threw back the remainder of his orange juice and got up from the table with his half-eaten food. "Excuse me."

His parents immediately halted their fighting to look at him.

"Wait, wait," his mother said. She looked across the table to her soon-to-be ex-husband. "We shouldn't be fighting."

His dad nodded and even reached for the dish of scrambled eggs to serve himself another ladle full.

"Also, we have something to ask you two," his mom said, without breaking eye contact with her estranged husband.

He stopped and braced himself.

"Your dad and I would like for you both to say a few words at the divorce party."

Duncan huffed. He'd somehow blocked out that impending event. It had been his mother's idea. She'd seen a segment about the trend on a morning talk show. Surprisingly, their father had gone along with it. It might've been the first time they'd agreed.

"Say something?" Gwen asked.

"Yeah, like a speech," their father replied. "Nothing too long."

Duncan rubbed the bridge of his nose. He'd barely

committed to showing up to the contrived party. "What would we even say?"

Their father lifted his heavy shoulders in a shrug. "Whatever you want. Keep it celebratory. Keep it light."

Celebratory and light. They were still trying to perform a lie.

His mother touched his arm. "Think about it."

He'd managed as much as he could of this brunch, and there were a dozen things left to do for the day. "I should get going."

———

Retta had re-downloaded a meditation app, and it was working. Despite her canceled date being in rescheduling purgatory, she was taking it in stride. Her water heater still sounded like the percussion section of a junior high jazz band, but she was unfazed.

Even the pending engagement party and wedding day elicited renewed energy to actually find someone to go with instead of anxiety.

As Retta helped the next customer in line, she resolved to get more serious about dates. She needed to expand her pool and carve out time to actually go out.

She hadn't been this strategic about her love life since she was a preteen. But if Retta went with the flow now, she risked showing up to Irene's festivities without anybody.

When the line thinned out, Retta took it as an opportunity to offer the patrons sitting inside her store some samples. Picking up the tray, she made her way through her bakery apologizing once again about the noisy water heater.

"It's our new shortbread cookies with blood orange caramel sauce," Retta said.

The women on their lunch breaks studied the offering and took one each.

It was on this little journey that Retta noticed a woman who was obviously some sort of social media influencer.

The beautiful young woman casually took a bite of a croissant and posed as a man across from her snapped a picture with a professional camera. Once the photo was taken, she spat out the piece she'd bitten.

Sure, it would be easy to make fun of such a display, but Retta refused to hate on anyone's hustle. The woman had paid for the various treats in front of her after all, and she'd tag Dutch Oven in the eventual posts she'd upload.

Returning to her spot behind the counter, Retta continued to study the influencer's photoshoot.

"I once tried to do the social media thing," Cheyenne said, also watching the scene play out. "A girl from my high school started a YouTube channel when we were sopho-mores and now she's rich. People buy t-shirts with her face on it. I quit after six months. It was too much work."

"I don't doubt it," Retta said.

In the next set up, the photographer's hand was in the frame. The woman grasped it and smiled at the camera adoringly. The narrative was clear: she was in a fabulous, wonderful, absolutely superb bakery with a boyfriend or a date.

However, based on how quickly they pulled their hands from each other once the photo was taken, Retta wondered if that was true at all.

"I don't think they're actually a couple," Retta said.

Cheyenne shrugged. "Does it matter? As long as it looks that way to her followers."

"I guess," Retta said.

That's what I need.

She internally chuckled at the absurd idea of totting a

guy around at the wedding who was only pretending to be her boyfriend. Even though it would definitely clear up the mental space this damn wedding was occupying, and there'd also be no emotional investment in some long-term future.

"I even heard there were agencies now that you can hire extras to pose in your content," Cheyenne continued.

Yeah with all the disposable income Retta was rolling in, she was totally going to rent a boyfriend. She'd stick to the dating apps and the disappointments she was used to.

Cheyenne left her then to clear vacated tables as Retta helped customers who'd walked in.

After processing a payment, she looked up to see Duncan step inside the bakery. His stature filled the door and his presence drew several eyes to him.

"Hi," he said, walking up to the counter.

She straightened her apron. This was it. She could feel it. "You here about the parking lot?"

"I am."

"Perfect," she said, grabbing a glass of water for him and motioning toward a table in the far corner of the store, right behind the croissant-spitting influencer.

Once they were seated, she watched him place his arms corded in muscles on the table. They took up the majority of the space, and it felt, even if unintentional, like a gesture of dominance. She straightened in her chair and squared her shoulders.

"The last thing we want to do is start a rivalry here," Duncan began.

Retta nodded. "Agreed."

"We get that there's a parking system in place, but…"

Why "but"? No "but".

"The fair thing to do, in our opinion, would be sharing the spaces," Duncan said.

Was it irrational and immature that her instinct in that moment was to perch on the table and screech, "mine"?

"Okay," Retta said, after taking several long breaths. She could be an adult about this. "What do you have in mind?"

"We could—"

"Excuse me," the social media influencer said as she bumped into the back of Duncan's seat trying to get up.

Tables and chairs shuffled as they made room for the woman to leave her seat.

Before exiting the bakery, the young woman shook her photographer slash pretend boyfriend's hand, and Retta found amusement in it all over again.

"Where were we?" Duncan asked.

Turning back to him to answer, Retta opened her mouth. However, nothing came out because she was struck silent by the halo surrounding Duncan's head, courtesy of the perfectly positioned sun behind him, and with it, the answer to her problems. It was as if a deity herself had whispered the solution to her.

Wait. No. She couldn't... Could she?

The pounding of her heart prevented her from scripting the conversation in her head. She gave up trying and said, "I have something really random to ask you. And if you hate it or think it's weird, we never have to bring it up again—"

"I'm good at forgetting, remember?" he said, taking a drink of water.

She took a breath. "Do you have a girlfriend?"

Duncan jerked forward, almost spewing water all over himself.

"I mean are you dating anyone right now? Retta asked.

Wiping his mouth with the back of his hand, he said, "I understood your question the first time." He closed his eyes momentarily and shook his head. "Are you asking me out?"

Retta looked around. "No. Kind of. My cousin's getting married."

"Okay?" Duncan said. "Congrats to her."

"Yes. Well, I need a date for the wedding…"

She hoped he'd fill in the blanks, understand the implications, and save her from spelling out this bizarre request.

Folding his arms, he frowned and said, "I'm confused. Are you suggesting I date you for parking spots?"

"W-we wouldn't actually be a couple. I need to show up at this wedding with someone."

"So, you want me to be your fake boyfriend?"

Hearing the request out loud was strange and humbling. She nodded.

"Why?" he asked.

"Does it matter?" Her ego wouldn't handle her exposing the reason why she was attending this wedding. She was already internally wilting from what she'd shared.

"Yeah, it matters. I don't make it a habit to blatantly lie to people."

Retta straightened her glasses. His words felt like an indictment against her, but she internally scrambled for a way to explain herself.

"You know when you're haunted by an embarrassing moment from years ago or an ugly yearbook photo, and all you want is a reset? To assure yourself and others that person isn't you? This wedding is my reset," she said.

Duncan's eyes narrowed, most likely because he was trying to decipher what the hell she was saying. "What happened to—what's his name—Steve?" he asked.

"I haven't seen him since our first date."

"After you asked him to be your fake boyfriend?"

Oh, this was a mistake. "You know what? Never mind," Retta said, moving to stand up.

Duncan stopped her by saying, "I'll do it for all three parking spots."

Shaking her head, Retta settled back in her seat. She had to think about her staff. "The best I can do is offer you one spot free and clear."

"Two," he countered.

"One and we can alternate the remaining two monthly," she said.

He was silent for such a long time before saying, "Add the recipe for the blueberry scones and it's a deal."

———

"Let me get this straight," Anthony said, holding up hitting pads for Duncan to punch. "You go over there to negotiate parking spaces and you come back with a girlfriend?"

"*Fake* girlfriend," Duncan said, increasing the speed and power of his punches. "I also got us reasonable parking and a scone recipe."

Despite pressure from his business partner to negotiate for a first-come, first-serve policy, Duncan thought it was a wrong strategy. He knew the parking was important to Retta as well, so he hadn't wanted to push too hard and wreck a business relationship.

After several minutes, Duncan backed away and caught his breath, leaning over the top rope of the ring.

"So, you're supposed to attend a wedding and an engagement party and pretend like she's your girl?" Anthony asked.

"Why is this so hard for you to wrap your head around."

"Because Duncan Gilmore voluntarily entered a relationship."

"Fake relationship," Duncan said, taking a drink of water. "You don't think I can pull it off?"

Anthony screwed his face. "Your longest relationship—if you want to call it that—lasted what? Three months?"

"It's called acting. None of it'll be real."

"Acting? You need to let go of that high school *Midsummer Night's Dream* rejection, brother," Anthony said.

"Man, fuck you," Duncan said, laughing.

"You also know nothing about her. How are you going to play a convincing boyfriend?"

"We have a *date*," Duncan said, placing heavy air quotes around the word date. "That should be enough for us to get to know each other and make us seem like a real couple in front of her family."

His friend shook his head, exasperated. "Do you hear yourself? I'll let this parking thing go and release you from this ridiculous plan." Anthony touched each of Duncan's shoulders like he was knighting him.

"I gave her my word, and besides it works out for both of us."

He wasn't completely sure of the reasons Retta wanted him to pose as her boyfriend at her cousin's wedding. But if he had to guess, he would say she wanted to ward off questions about her relationship status.

His sister often complained about the questions and comments she'd receive from different family members about getting married. He got them too, but they were never laced with judgment or condescension.

"Wait, do you want to sleep with her or something? Is this some long game to endear yourself to her?" Anthony asked, clapping his padded hands together before positioning them for Duncan to hit.

He dropped his head backward for a moment. "No, because there're less complicated ways to get laid."

In fact, he'd be looking into those ways as soon as this arrangement with Retta was over.

"She's beautiful, but this is strictly business," Duncan said before throwing a punch.

Chapter Six

WHAT STRUCK Duncan when he entered the bowling alley, the site of his "date" with Retta, was how few people were in there. The only other patrons were a group of forty-somethings who were singing along to the muffled 2000s pop music playing from the speakers above. He chose to ignore the feet and onion ring smell that also drifted through the building.

After getting his shoes and assigned a lane, he waited only a few minutes before Retta arrived as well.

"You look great," Duncan said, taking in her breezy countenance.

"Oh!" She looked down at her jeans and a flowy blouse. "It's old. I stole it from my friend's closet."

He wanted to say more about it. Flirt a little bit, but he didn't know if that was allowed. There wasn't exactly a guidebook on how to fake date.

"This is for you," Duncan said, handing her a wrapped square package.

Her eyes widened as she took a hold of it. "I didn't get you anything."

"It's honestly nothing," he said. This was a weird situation, and he felt like maybe this might ease the awkwardness. But now he was second-guessing the logic.

She unwrapped the small gift to reveal colorful Post-it notes. The same ones she'd been leaving on his and the team's cars for the past weeks.

Retta cracked a smile, and he relaxed a bit.

"I thought you might've been running low," he said.

She smiled even wider and shook her head. "Thank you." After placing the bundle in her purse, she said, "I was thinking we could start with some ice breakers."

Smart. It would make them comfortable talking to each other. "Hit me," he said, stepping up onto the raised platform closer to her.

Adjusting her glasses with the tips of her fingers, she looked down at her phone. "Last name?"

"Gilmore."

"Majors," she offered.

She then asked his age.

"Twenty-nine," he said after the noise from the rowdy group bowling beside them died down.

"Twenty-eight."

He nodded, trying not to betray how amusing he found having questions launched at him as if he were at a job interview.

"What did you want to be when you were younger?" Retta read from her screen.

"A school teacher. My whole family are teachers. That's how my parents met actually."

She opened her mouth like she might have a follow-up question, but instead she said, "I wanted to be an artist."

Before *he* could find out more, she queried about something else.

He realized after another three questions, she'd be

content to do this for their entire date and that certainly wouldn't happen on his watch. He wasn't going to spend his one day off answering prompts that, at best, would help unlock his dormant Facebook account.

"If you could be an animal—"

"Hey, hey," he gently said. She looked up at him over the brim of her glasses and for the briefest of moments, something in his stomach caught.

"What?" she asked.

Clearing his throat, he said, "We should maybe get in a little bowling seeing that we're here."

She looked up and around them as if she'd in fact forgotten where they were. "Right," she said, tossing her phone onto her purse. "I'll warn you, the last time I played I was twelve."

"We're in the same boat," Duncan said as he stretched his shoulders and rotated his neck. "But we're only playing a friendly game."

Walking over to their lane, Retta sort of curtsied and released the ball she'd picked up. It landed straight in the gutter.

He clapped. "That's okay."

She muttered something then squared her shoulders before sending the next one down the lane. This time, she was able to eliminate all the pins save for two.

They swapped places, and he stepped up to the front and bowled. His ball only clipped the side of one pin before miserably falling into the gutter. The next bowl was far worse. The uncooperative sphere landed in the damned trench almost immediately after he released it from his hand.

"Warmup round," Duncan said as he and Retta passed each other.

It proved true for Retta because she hit a strike and a

spare on her next two turns. Duncan, on the other hand, failed to get more than three pins to fall. While he was on a mediocre streak, Retta continued to get excellent scores to the point where Duncan was impressed with her skill but worried that he'd lost all his athletic ability between the time he'd woken up and now.

After a particularly bad bowl, Duncan turned around to find Retta fighting a smile.

"What?"

"You're throwing it like you're trying to make craters in the floor," she said.

Damn. He looked back to where he'd bowled.

She laughed. It was high pitched and staccato, and the most captivating thing. It was also the first time he'd ever seen her truly relaxed.

Advancing toward her, he said, "So, all I'm hearing is I have massive biceps, and my strength is my weakness."

"Sure," she said, giving his arms an impassive look. "Or you just suck at bowling."

He raised one brow. "That's a challenge if I ever heard one."

"No. As you said, we're playing a friendly game… that I'm winning."

She tossed her straightened hair fashioned in a half updo over her shoulder. "My turn."

Would the fake dating guidebook consider any of this flirting? Maybe. But he'd have to get props for ignoring the way she would pull her jeans up by the belt loops before each bowl. Her thighs would jiggle some, and when she'd bend down her ass would—

Okay, so maybe he was paying more attention than he'd care to admit.

When it was his turn once again, he was determined to have a gentler hand while rolling the ball. It worked, and he received his highest score yet. Retta responded by patting his arm like he was some puppy who'd managed not to eat his own shit. She went on to score another strike.

"Last time I bowled I was twelve, my ass," he said, watching her saunter back.

Raising her hands, she said, "I promise you I'm as shocked as you are."

It didn't matter for too long, however, because after a few more rounds they were neck and neck. He pumped his fist on his way back to the plastic chairs.

"Remind me never to give you advice," she said as she looked at their even scores before heading back up.

"That's not good sportsmanship," he said as she readied to send a ball down.

Unfortunately, before she released it, Duncan happened to cough. The disruption resulted in a skewed bowl.

"You did that on purpose," she said, coming right up to him.

"I didn't," he said. But the laugh he released in response to her overly serious expression, undermined his statement. "I don't need to cheat to win."

She squinted and studied him before saying, "Of course not. Good luck."

Picking up a ball, he geared up for his throw.

"I want you to feel confident," Retta shouted from behind. "You can do this."

He looked over his shoulder at her, seeing right through the mind game she was playing.

"Come on, roll the ball," she said, giving him two thumbs up.

His preoccupation with what Retta might do resulted in abysmal bowls. Meeting her where she stood, he said, "So, you wanna play dirty, huh?"

She lightly pressed her finger into his chest. "You started it."

Instinctually he grabbed her finger.

Her eyes widened, and she looked at where he held her and back to his face. He'd never dated anyone this tall, but he decided he liked that she could easily meet his eye.

"It's on, Majors," he said, before releasing her.

"I'm ready."

But before they could find out how this newly inspired vigor would play out, jarring beeps rang through the bowling alley.

He and Retta jumped back and looked around them. The other patrons similarly searched for answers, but all Duncan could offer was a shrug.

A short man in his sixties emerged from an office behind the front desk. Duncan, Retta, and the group beside them watched as the man took steps in tempo with the lethargic beeping sounds toward the other corner of the large room.

A minute later he arrived at his destination, and the noise stopped soon after. However, they didn't have a chance to relax or get back to bowling before the older man bellowed from his spot inside the room, "Meredith, it's fucked!"

In unison, everyone whipped their heads to the only other person working.

The older woman at the front desk didn't look up from her computer when she shouted, "You sure?"

Everyone turned to look at the door the man had disappeared behind.

"Yeah, I'm sure!"

Eyes back on Meredith.

The woman visibly sighed before standing up, retrieving a megaphone on the shelf behind her and positioning it over her mouth. "Folks, if I could get everyone's attention." She scanned the room for several seconds.

God knows why. The nine of them were silent and waiting.

"We're having some technical difficulties, so we're shutting down the lanes for the rest of the evening."

"Wait, are you joking?" someone from the group next to them asked.

Meredith, with a bored expression, looked over to the man who'd spoken. "In an orderly fashion, you can approach the desk to collect your shoes and a refund if you choose."

The older woman then returned to her seat and continued to do what she was doing behind the computer. Meanwhile, the lights illuminating the lanes dimmed and the screens where their scores were tracked shut down.

Everyone retrieved their belongings and left the building mumbling their disappointment.

Retta was in her purse, fishing for her keys when she said, "I promise I checked the reviews for this place. They were decent."

"Well, on the bright side, you don't have to go home a loser," he said.

She laughed. "A little too confident for someone who spent half the time with balls in the gutter."

Her words were the last thing said before they both understood this "date" was over despite it only beginning. Maybe the rapport they'd built in the last hour and a half was enough to get them through the wedding events.

He shoved his hands into his pockets. "Send me the link to those questions. I'll send you back the answers," he said.

Retta nodded. "I'll do the same."

"Cool."

They both fell silent, and this was part of a date that would include a hug, perhaps a kiss. But he kept his hands where they were and waited for her to make a move. And she did, toward her car.

"See you later," she said.

And as he sat in his vehicle, he kept thinking how he'd been having fun while accomplishing the goal of getting to know her. She was still parked, and it was far from late.

"Screw it," he said to himself before opening his truck door.

———

Retta entered her car and took a full breath for the first time since the day had started. The malfunctioning bowling lanes had been her unintentional savior. This date should've been less stressful than a real one. She literally didn't have to be pretty, impressive, or even likable.

However, she'd been having fun. The sort of fun you'd over-analyze with friends afterward.

She'd thought they'd been flirting.

"You wanna play dirty, huh?"

But all this musing was particularly mortifying because this was the most enjoyable date she'd been on in a while, and it had to be fake. Shaking her head, she placed her keys in the ignition. A sharp knock sounded on the driver's side window before she could pull out.

Retta found Duncan standing there and was too thrown to think of what he might want as she rolled down the window.

"Do you have anywhere to be right now?" he asked.

"Ah, why?"

He rubbed the back of his neck and looked out to the road her car faced. "Well, our date was cut short, I'm starving, and the fair is in town. So, I was thinking if you have no place to be, we can head over there for an hour or two."

Despite the fair being her scene, Retta felt compelled to reject the invitation. Hadn't she told herself moments earlier that their limited interaction was enough?

Say no.

"Sure."

Chapter Seven

AFTER REALIZING public transportation would be their best option, Duncan and Retta dropped off their vehicles at their respective apartments and met each other at the fair. As they stood in the admittance line, Duncan watched as she barely made eye contact with him and swept her gaze across the crowd every so often. She might be nervous they'd bump into someone she knew, but he feared she'd chew her bottom lip off if he didn't distract her.

"You said you wanted to be an artist growing up," Duncan said as they took a few steps forward in the progressing queue. "What kind?"

Retta stopped scanning the area to look at him. "A painter. I was going to get my Bachelor of Fine Arts and everything."

"So, how did baking come in?" he asked, pleased to see her shoulders relax and faint smile lines appear.

"I was generally artistic and liked working with my hands. But baking wasn't something I even thought about until the summer before I was supposed to start college. I went to this French bakery in Seattle." Retta paused, looking at Duncan. "I know it sounds silly, but I sorta had this out of body experience when I tasted the croissants and brioche. I knew then and there that I wanted to learn to make things like that for as many people as possible."

"Doesn't sound silly at all," he said as they were called up to purchase their tickets. "You followed your gut."

Inside the fair, they found a robust crowd, food trucks, and noisy carnival rides and games. And once it was dark, Duncan knew the strung up lights would add more beauty to the scene.

"Where do you want to start?" he asked.

"Do you want to grab something to eat?"

He nodded, and they both assessed the food trucks parked close by.

"Let's try this one," Duncan said, pointing to one with the least amount of people in front of it.

"What do they sell?" Retta asked as they both squinted to make out the shabby chalkboard menu.

When they neared the front of the line, the words "deep-fried poutine balls" became clear.

"That sounds vile," she whispered, looking at him like he'd come up with the idea himself.

"We should at least give it a try. You don't get deep-fried poutine every—"

The person directly in front of them who'd received his order turned around and took an enormous bite out of the creation. The brown gravy oozed, dripping down his chin and into his beard. Any resemblance to the beloved Québécois dish had been lost in the process of breading and frying it.

"What can I get for you folks?" the attendant asked, peering from the small food truck window above.

"Nothing."

"We're good, thank you."

They said simultaneously.

Leaving the line as quickly as possible, they found a truck more in line with their tastes. They received their order of Mac N Cheese and pulled pork tacos and located a spare corner to stand and eat. The tangy slaw and the rich pork on the tacos were brightened with fresh avocado and cilantro. The macaroni wasn't bad either.

However, Duncan couldn't process what he was tasting once Retta softly grunted. He watched her tongue move across her bottom lip and the mechanics of her jaw and delicate throat. At one point, he stopped eating altogether because she closed her eyes and tipped her head back.

After her display of unintentional eroticism, she wiped her mouth with a napkin and asked, "You said your parents are both teachers?"

Duncan cleared his throat. "Yeah, all that pressure. They knew my teachers personally. Couldn't get away with shit."

"Are they still teaching?" Retta asked, smiling.

"My dad retired a few years ago, but my mom's still going. And, of course, my sister is a teacher as well. I kinda rebelled in that sense."

"What happened?" she asked.

"I got into boxing in high school, but I ended up training and competing on the side through college. I met Anthony at one of the gyms. I don't know if I would've had the guts to start the business without him."

"I'm sure your parents are proud," she said.

"I hope so."

"Is your dad anxiously waiting for your mom to retire? One of my uncles went back to work because he couldn't stand being in the house alone."

Duncan smiled wryly. "Nah, I think he's good, seeing they're getting a divorce and everything."

"Shit." Retta dropped her gaze. "I'm sorry. I shouldn't have assumed."

"Don't be sorry," he said, nabbing the last taco. He didn't want to dive into that conversation. It was better to quickly move on. "Let's see what else there's to eat."

———

It was a bona fide skill at this point how Retta could put her foot in her mouth when Duncan was around. She hated that she'd broached that particular subject at a carnival of all places. However, she was determined to not further mar their time together by harping on about the mistake.

After getting grilled pineapple on sticks, Retta and Duncan walked deeper into the fairgrounds. They passed carnival games whose rules could be summarized with: throw or hit a weird shaped object.

"Oh, a punching machine thing," Retta said, pointing at the contraption.

"Yeah, I don't think that's a good idea," Duncan said.

"Why? Your massive biceps?"

He laughed. "Exactly that."

"Fine, let me do it," she said as she got in line. "I want to get the big parrot plush toy. My niece is obsessed with birds right now."

"How old is she?"

"Six. And her brother is eight. Do you have the one sibling?"

"Yup, only Gwen and me. The coolest sister, by the way. How about you?" he asked.

"An older brother."

"Are you close?"

"We weren't that close growing up. Probably because I kept on crushing on his friends," Retta said, laughing.

As they got closer to the front, Retta studied people's techniques for throwing a punch.

"I think I can do better than that," she said under her breath.

"Do you want tips?" Duncan asked.

"Hell, yeah. Show me."

"Are you right-handed or left?" he asked, stepping closer.

She raised her right hand.

"Okay, place your right foot back and when you go to punch, rotate your hips and pivot your back foot," he said, demonstrating the movement. "It'll give you more power."

She imitated him.

"Now, let's see your fist."

When she presented her right clenched hand to him, he adjusted her thumb before giving a satisfactory nod. "Go ahead, Rocky."

Jabbing the air in front of her, she said, "You know, I've never actually watched *Rocky*."

Duncan stepped back like one of her punches had landed. "Never?"

His tone was so incredulous she decided to tease him. "Is it any good?"

"You've said all I need to know," he replied. "We're watching *Rocky*."

She didn't have the chance to ask him about this presumed second "date" they'd have because the woman running the game called out, "Ma'am, you're next."

Turning, she dumped her purse in Duncan's arms

before stepping up to the bag. With all her strength she hit the teardrop-shaped target. The bright red digits presented her decent score. It was higher than the three people before her. She looked at the attendant, hoping her slightly sore hand wouldn't be in vain.

"Congratulations, ma'am. You can pick anything from the third shelf."

Retta laughed. The bird was on the sixth one.

She shrugged as she approached Duncan with a small alligator plush toy. "I thought I did well."

He gave her back her purse, but before she could suggest a place to go next, he joined the line to hit the bag.

"What're you doing?" she asked.

"Getting you that bird."

Her breathing faltered. "You don't have to do that."

"I know."

When it was Duncan's turn to go, he drew his fist back and released what she suspected was only a portion of his kinetic energy into the bag. But the entire machine still freaked out. The numbers went all over the place and changed colors. She thought he might've broken it before a big number and the words "new high score" appeared.

Retta's lips parted.

The woman who managed the game looked Duncan up and down. "Congratulations. You can choose anything from the top shelf."

Duncan got the parrot and strode back to her with it. He looked so powerful. Like an action hero at the end of a movie, leaving a site seconds before an explosion went off behind him. He even carried the five-foot stuffed toy over his shoulder as one might carry a well-worn leather jacket.

"Thank you," she said as she accepted the surprisingly heavy plush animal and cleared her mind of the oddly specific visuals of him as a leading man.

They agreed to scope out the thrill rides visible in the distance. Along the way, they paused to watch different machines spin, sway, and plunge.

"You need help?" Duncan asked after she'd shifted the bird from one arm to the other a dozen times.

"Please," she said, heaving the toy toward him.

He looked the part of a boyfriend holding her stuffed animal. If she reached for his hand, it would complete the picture. Was this how he was like? He caught her studying him and raised his brows.

She hesitated for a moment then said, "I was wondering what your dating life looks like. When you're not fake dating someone, of course."

He smiled. "It's regular. Fun. I'm not big on anything too serious."

She made a contemplative sound, refusing to ask what the "fun" he spoke of entailed. Oh, she could easily guess, but hearing it from his mouth might be her undoing.

"And you? How's your love life when you're not fake dating someone?" he asked. "Of course."

Awkwardness clawed up Retta's back. Though she'd literally started this line of questioning, she felt the same way when certain family members discussed her singledom like she was a subject in a research study.

"Well, I'm the one who solicited you to be my fake boyfriend, so I'd say not good."

Before he could comment on her statement, she pointed up. "Let's try this one."

She and Duncan stopped in front of a thrill ride where the screams of the people on it were the loudest. Roller coasters were not her favorite thing, but they always left her exhilarated.

"I'm down," he said.

After fifteen minutes of waiting, they were escorted to

adjacent seats. She jostled the over-the-shoulder restraints a few times to make sure it was secure and let out a long breath.

Turning to Duncan, she expected to find him pumped and excited, but he looked almost gray.

"You okay?" she asked.

He looked at her. "Yeah, just nervous."

Though Retta knew fear wasn't limited to certain kinds of people, seeing Duncan anxious heightened her nerves. "We can get off." She was already looking around for help.

He shook his head. "I'm good. But you never know with these things."

"Why would you say that now?" she asked, tightening her grip around the handles on the seat.

The robotic voice reciting the rules of the ride now sounded ominous as their carriers began a slow ascent. Her heartbeat right along with it.

The moment their chairs pitched forward, Duncan and Retta's hands instinctively found each other's. Without her glasses, she couldn't clearly see the parking lot below or the buildings in the distance, and it inspired her to chant a prayer.

Duncan laughed nervously a moment before their chairs went absolutely still.

"God, are we stuck?" she squealed.

Her words turned into a scream when their rotating chairs of death plummeted toward the earth. If that wasn't stomach turning enough, they were flipped and twirled through the air, and by the time all of it had ended Retta was grateful they hadn't eaten more than they had.

Once they returned to solid ground, they sat there until their seatbelts were released with a loud whoosh. They looked at each other, grinning. This feeling made the turbulence worth it.

Their hands remained intertwined as they got up, and all of Retta's senses and attention migrated there. It took stepping off the podium, collecting their belongings, and returning to the fairgrounds for them to separate.

"Do you want to try another one or do something else?" Duncan asked.

"I kinda want to know what's happening over there," she said as she pointed to an area where people gathered around a slightly raised stage.

A sign said a show would start in five minutes.

"Very informative," Duncan said of the cryptic message.

While they waited amongst the audience for their curiosity to be satisfied, Retta's initial anxieties about being at the fair were realized when someone said, "Oh, my God, Retta?"

She turned and quickly put a foot between her and Duncan. "Claire!"

Retta's unease at seeing her fellow baker and friend had nothing to do with the woman herself but rather how unprepared she was to debut Duncan as her boyfriend. She and Claire were two Black women in the same industry, and they'd always been friendly and supportive of each other's careers. To the extent that Claire had been one of the handful of people who'd reached out when Retta dealt with her professional setback.

"Hold on, I need to give you a hug," her friend said as she got closer. "I haven't seen you in ages."

"I know. I thought you were out east," Retta said.

"We moved back late last year. Louis," she pointed to her husband whom Retta had met a few times before, "got a job here."

Her husband was preoccupied with talking to a small group of people.

"That's great. We'll have to grab coffee soon and catch up," Retta said.

"Yes, of course," Claire said, eyeing Duncan who still stood near her.

Well, now she had no other choice but to make introductions. "Duncan, this is my friend, Claire. Claire, this is Duncan. My…"

The word "boyfriend" lodged in Retta's throat. She pressed her lips together to make the sound of the first consonant, but all that came out was a pathetic whistle.

Thankfully, Duncan stepped forward and said, "Hey, nice to meet you."

"Same here," Claire said.

They all stood there nodding and looking at one another, and Retta made no effort to foster a conversation between the two because that would undoubtedly lead to questions.

"By the way, your t-shirt's dope," Duncan said.

Claire's eyes widened. "You're a fan?"

"Since day one."

"Really? Oh, my God. My husband and I host viewing parties. If you're ever interested let me know. Retta, you have my email, right?"

She nodded, but they didn't seem to notice her response because the two of them were already engaging in a rapid conversation about some sci-fi TV show. They didn't let up for several minutes.

"Wow, it was really nice meeting you," Claire said to Duncan, smiling.

"Yeah, and I'll definitely check out that podcast."

Claire and Retta hugged once again before she left to rejoin Louis.

"I think we did pretty well for our first time," Duncan said.

"You did great. I, on the other hand——"

Retta froze as she felt the undeniable wetness of a rain-drop on her face. She looked up at the sky as dark, bloated clouds rolled in. "It's going to rain." She immediately placed her purse over her head and looked around for cover.

Duncan took her hand and quickly led her to a small space between two carnival game stations somewhat covered by a decorative canopy. It was a good thing too, because the moment they settled into the tight space, it started to pour. It was like the rain had a point to make and sidewalks to clean.

They watched as people similarly ran for cover or left the fairgrounds all together. Claire and her husband made a beeline for the exit.

"The busses are gonna be packed," Duncan said, his rich voice coiling around her.

Whether it was because of the sudden chill in the air or Duncan's closeness, Retta nipples stiffened. Closing her arms around herself, she willed them to go down.

"You're cold," he said, his eyebrows stitched close together.

Her stomach fluttered at the thought of him drawing her flush to his chest and locking her in his embrace. It definitely wouldn't help her situation.

"No, it's fine," she said, giving him a small smile.

Must. Not. Lean. In.

"I saw a restaurant across the street," she said. "We can wait out the rain there, and the busses won't be so congested either."

"Let's do it," he said. While holding the bird plushie, he removed his jacket and handed it to her. "For your hair."

She placed the garment over her head, feeling his body heat emanating from it. "Thank you."

"You ready?" he asked, holding out his hand.

She nodded, placing her hand into his before they started running.

Chapter Eight

THEY ARRIVED at the Western-themed restaurant drenched and out of breath.

"I can't believe we did that," Retta said between airy laughter.

Duncan turned toward her to make a comment but was winded all over again. Her once flowy blouse clung to her body, molding around her small breasts and revealing her obviously hard nipples.

"Fuck."

He didn't realize he'd said the expletive out loud until Retta looked up from where she'd been trying to clear the fog from her glasses.

Duncan quickly held up the poor parrot plushie, traumatized from their journey.

She laughed, returning her glasses to her face. "Nothing a good blow dryer can't fix."

A young waiter named Graham approached and didn't seem concerned with their physical state when he asked, "Together?"

The two of them looked at each other. "Yes."

It was a benign inquiry, but with their answer, they'd stepped further into the ruse of their relationship.

The waiter led them past oversized booths and a stack of hay bales to the back of the mostly empty restaurant. Once seated, Duncan used napkins on the table to wipe the rain from his skin. Retta's pressed hair had somewhat survived and she'd taken to hypnotically flapping the neckline of her blouse in a futile attempt to dry it.

"Did he look convinced when we said we were together?" Retta asked after a moment.

"I don't think he cares enough," Duncan replied before taking a long drink from the glass of water their server had left for them. "Why? You worried?"

"I couldn't even call you my boyfriend in front of a friend I've only known for a few years. That's a problem because my family, my meddling, eagle-eyed family? Will notice."

Duncan spotted Graham walking back to their table. "Okay, let's practice."

"What—"

"Are you ready to order?" Graham asked, poised with a pen and a notepad.

Duncan sat up straight and said, "Yes, I'll get any tea that's decaf, and my *girlfriend* here will get…"

Retta's eyes widened, and she looked between their waiter and him before saying, "I'll get the same as my *boyfriend*."

Graham's gaze flicked upward. "Coming right up."

"See, not bad," Duncan said when they were alone.

"Except it sounds like we're reading from a teleprompter."

"We're practicing," he said, spinning the massive menus on the table around and around. "What about terms of endearment? Which ones do you like?"

"Any but the ones that are food related. Suga, pumpkin, muffin. You'd be surprised how many people randomly started using those when I became a baker."

Their waiter returned with their tea before Duncan could reassure her that those weren't his style.

"Here, you go," Graham said, sliding the cups and teapot in front of them. "Careful. The water is hot."

"Baby, do you want any sugar?" Duncan asked, taking hold of Retta's hand on a whim.

She pressed her lips together before saying, "No, babe, I'm good."

"Uh-ah. Right," Graham said after a long pause. "Just so you know, you'll have to order actual food if you're going to stay."

The waiter left them to decide, and Duncan opened the large menu. There were too many dissonant choices. At first, he thought the restaurant served Italian food, but Japanese dishes were included halfway down the second page and Mediterranean items on the next.

"This menu is exhausting," Retta said, slapping the book shut. "Do you want to share an order of fries or something?"

"I'm cool with that," he said as he continued to scan the humorously confused menu. He didn't think it could get better until he read the promotional blurb for a contest the restaurant held on a rolling basis.

He looked up at Retta. "Would you do a cake eating challenge?"

"What?" she asked.

He turned the menu and pointed to the section.

She frowned. "You want to do that right now?"

"Yeah, why not?"

"I don't know. Nausea, bloating, drowsiness—"

"But think about the glory."

Retta rolled her eyes, but when their waiter returned for their orders, she asked, "Could you tell us more about the cake eating competition?"

"If you can finish the whole cake in twenty-five minutes between the two of you, you won't have to pay for it. You'll also get tickets to our annual seafood event, a hundred dollars in cash, and we match that amount to the local children's hospital."

Duncan looked at Retta. "See, a good cause."

"How many people have won?" Retta asked.

Graham pointed to a wall at the corner of the restaurant with mounted picture frames. "A couple dozen. We've been doing this since 2012."

Retta shook her head before saying to Duncan, "You're carrying me out of here if I pass out from a sugar rush."

"I got you," Duncan said before clapping his hands and rubbing them together. "Bring it on, Graham."

———

Within ten minutes, their server returned with the cake. He settled it between them, and Retta studied the monstrous dessert covered with white buttercream and confetti sprinkles.

The whole date had been a sequence of odd events, but this was something she would never typically think of doing with someone she didn't even consider a friend. However, Duncan's exuberance was contagious.

"Why am I nervous?" Retta asked, presenting her shaking hands for Duncan to see. "I feel like we're about to go on another roller coaster."

Also, her ego was now somehow tied to how fast she could eat cake.

"We got this," he said, raising his hand for a high five that she responded to.

With his thumb poised on the stopwatch, Graham asked, "Are you folks ready?"

They nodded.

"You can begin eating now."

Retta grabbed the knife and server they'd been provided and cut herself a slice.

Meanwhile, Duncan went straight into the cake with his fork. "We don't have time to be refined here."

She placed a forkful of cake in her mouth, and the corners of her lips turned down as she chewed. Leaning forward, she whispered, "It's dry."

"This isn't about that. You get it down," Duncan said. His shoulders were hunched, and his movements mechanical.

In an attempt to match his pace and vigor, Retta forked an even bigger piece into her mouth but almost choked. The cake went down as smoothly as sawdust. Mercifully, they'd also been given tall glasses of milk. For several minutes, they took graceless bites and washed it down with their drinks. If her mother could see her now.

"I think I like this buttercream though. It's not too sweet," Retta said, as she paused to study it on her fork. Concentrating on the details and technique put into the construction of the cake, helped her forget her suffering.

Duncan snapped his fingers and pointed at their sugary burden. "Focus."

"You have thirteen minutes left," Graham said. He'd settled onto a stool and split his time between his phone and watching them eat.

Retta and Duncan looked at the amount of cake left and then to each other. Without breaking eye contact, they plunged their fists into the tiered structure and shoved a chunk of it into their mouths. Hey, they had tickets to an annual seafood event to win.

———

Why had he even thought this was a good idea?

After many minutes, Duncan slowed down, shaking his head. "I can't do this."

"One minute," Graham said.

Their waiter's pronouncement gave Duncan a second wind. He started tapping the table to the rhythm of his chewing and mentally blocking out any discomfort.

Graham raised his arm and held out his fingers as he said, "Ten, Nine."

One lopsided slice left.

"Eight, seven."

His mouth was full, and he thought he might hurl.

"Six, five."

Retta suddenly stood up and stomped her feet like she was trying to force the food down.

"Four, three."

He'd never eat cake again. Fuck cake. It was the worst thing in this world. Too sweet. Overrated.

"Two, One."

Both him and Retta turned to Graham and stuck their tongues out and shouted, "Ah!"

Had they eaten enough? There were still crumbs and icing left over. Would that disqualify them? They couldn't have gotten this far only to pay ninety bucks for such a torturous experience.

"You can put your tongues away," Graham said, moving closer to the table. He studied the cake stand for several seconds before looking back at his clipboard. He stroked his chin, mumbled a few things, then looked up at them. "Congratulations, you won."

Duncan turned to Retta with wide eyes and threw his hands in the air. They laughed and embraced only to immediately recoil when they hit each other's stomachs. After he was sure he wouldn't throw up all over the floor, he straightened from where he'd been leaning on a table. He found Retta laying across an empty booth with her eyes closed and cake smudged on her glasses.

Graham returned with more napkins and a pitcher of water. "So, whenever you're ready, we'll take a photo and collect your information."

Duncan cleaned himself up before walking over to a depleted Retta and nudging her foot with his. "You still with me?"

She stretched out her hand. "Help me."

He pulled her until she was seated upright.

"We're a hundred dollars richer," she said.

Once she'd wiped the frosting from her face and hands, they made their way to the wall of fame.

"Folks usually do a fun pose," Graham said, pointing to the frames with pictures of people jumping in the air, standing on the bar, and riding piggyback.

The two of them shuffled around each other, lifted their arms, and twisted their bodies, trying to find a suitable position.

"Why don't I dip you?" Duncan asked.

"That's fine," she said, eliminating almost all the space between them.

He didn't breathe as she wrapped both arms around his torso. When he placed his hand on her back, the heat of her skin traveled past the thin blouse she wore. This was the closest they'd ever been.

"Don't drop me," she whispered.

Duncan moved her backward and bent into his left leg. "No chance."

She flinched, but after several seconds of hovering over the floor at an angle, her face broke into a smile.

After the photo had been taken and forms signed, Retta held up their little Dollar Store trophy. "Your glory, sir."

They each gave the long-suffering waiter a hearty handshake and a tip before returning to their seats for their belongings. The rain had stopped, but he couldn't be sure when it had happened.

"I don't think we'll be catching any busses," Retta said, holding up her phone to show it was a little past eleven.

When their Uber arrived, they shoved themselves and the human-sized bird plushie into the back seat. It was nearly impossible for them to sit without physical contact. Her leg was practically in his lap, and he had to swing his arm over her headrest to make more room.

He forced himself to watch the lights of the city run together in a kaleidoscopic haze to avoid looking at her. It was the only way he could ignore her weight against his body.

But the strategy was abandoned when Retta turned to him and said, "You smell like cake."

She was so close. It would take but a slight tilt forward for him to kiss her. "You do too."

Laughing, she sunk deeper into the seat. "I'm glad this went well."

"I was nervous there for a second with your sketchy bowling alley," he said, closing his fist against the sudden desire to play with her hair that tickled his forearm.

She smiled at him and playfully elbowed his side. They should've looked away then and finished the trip in amiable silence, but her smile faded as their gazes remained locked. He leaned in, beckoned by the heat of her body and the sweet scent of her skin. At this point, he didn't care what his hypothetical fake dating guidebook would say, he wanted to kiss her.

And he would have done it, if she hadn't, in the next instant, licked his right cheek. The droning radio was the only distinguishable sound for many seconds.

"Ah, you had frosting," she said, fidgeting with her glasses.

He nodded like it was a sensible explanation and as if his heart wasn't racing. The cogs in his brain ground to a halt, and he couldn't formulate a response before the car pulled up in front of her apartment complex.

Retta pushed her door open and slipped out with the bird plushie in hand. "Sorry about the…" She touched her face. "Have a good night."

She walked through the security door and disappeared within the building. He was so caught up replaying what had happened, he almost missed it when the driver asked, "Where to next, sir?"

Chapter Nine

SITTING IN KYM'S KITCHEN, Retta swiped some raisins from a bowl on the counter. It was safe to say her friend had officially entered nesting mode. The living room had baby gear in different stages of construction, stacks of books crowded the dining table, and the house had already been baby proofed. Retta had offered to help her get organized, but she was having none of it.

"How're things with Steve?" Kym asked as she removed her second tray of cookies from the oven.

It took several seconds for Retta to remember who the hell Steve was. Why did it feel like a lifetime ago?

Retta cleared her throat. "Ah, he ghosted me."

Her friend spun around with a glob of cookie dough in her hand. "Asshole. I'm sorry."

"It's fine."

"That doesn't bode well for your 'sexy date for my cousin's wedding who happens to be marrying my ex-boyfriend' mission," Kym said.

"We should workshop that title."

"Really? I think it rolls off the tongue," Kym said,

shrugging. "So, what's next? Do I need to take time off after all?"

"You mean to give birth? Yeah, probably," Retta said, staring pointedly at her friend's belly. "Don't worry about me. I've got it figured out."

Kym squinted and pointed a spatula at Retta like a sword. "What're you not telling me?"

Retta took another handful of raisins to emote casualness and effortlessness before she said, "I'm kinda seeing someone."

Her friend's arm dropped. "That's great."

She nodded, but before she could reveal the whole truth, a voice from the front of Kym's house said, "Hey, sorry I'm late."

The distinct click of heels was detectable before their friend Nia fully entered the room in a short dress that swung about her curvy body.

"Who knew you can develop a fear of driving after not doing it for months?" Nia asked as she set her expensive purse and two brightly colored shopping bags on the chair.

Nia's life was particularly glamorous, think Fashion Week and other gigs that took her all around the world.

Retta often thought she was busy and barely keeping it together, but seeing her friend somehow manage a hectic schedule while still wearing high heels, kept her grateful that she could at least wear Crocs to work.

"Oh my God, you're so pregnant," Nia said, going over to Kym to hug her and marvel at her growing midsection.

"Forget about my big ass belly. Those shoes," Kym said pointing at Nia's stilettos.

Nia kicked up her heel. "These? They were sent to me last month. Speaking of the perks of my job…" She retrieved the bags she'd entered with and handed each of them one.

"Babe, you didn't have to," Kym said, already pulling the pretty tissue paper apart to reveal a beautiful cashmere baby blanket, sweater, and hat set.

Retta found a lovely pair of small hoop earrings that she gaped at for a while before asking, "Girl, how much did these cost?"

Nia waved them off. "I told you, perks of the job."

They all hugged before Kym asked, "How was your trip?"

"Oh, a delayed flight, lost luggage, and a runway show that was an absolute fail, but I'm off to Cape Town soon, so that's exciting."

Retta looked up, noting the weariness in her friend's voice. And now that she was paying attention, she could see the bags under her eyes. All the perfectly applied makeup in the world couldn't hide that. Kym and Retta exchanged a look.

"Don't burn out, okay?" Kym said, placing another tray of dough into the oven.

"Impossible. I'm living my dream," Nia said, laughing. "But enough about me. I've missed you guys. What's been going on?"

"Well," Kym said, taking the hint that Nia no longer wanted to be bugged about her horrendous work-life balance. "Len and I finally agreed that we'd hyphenate the baby's last name. It didn't sit right with me to give our child his last name when we're not even married."

"Oh, I like that idea. And your last names are short enough," Nia said as she reached for a cookie on the cooling rack. She narrowly missed hitting the light fixture above the island with her intricately styled faux locs.

"Also, Ret's seeing someone."

"What?" Nia said, jerking her head to look at Retta. "Who?"

"He owns the boxing gym next door to Dutch," Retta said. "But—"

"An athlete?" Kym asked, her eyes widened. "That's a choice."

Kym's college boyfriend had been a football player. She had feelings about it.

"Wait," Nia said, drawing out the word. "The gym you were complaining about a couple of weeks ago?"

"Yeah," Retta said, looking between her friends. There really wasn't a graceful way to relay the next piece of information. She just had to come out and say it. "But our relationship is, one might say, unconventional? We made an agreement that he'll attend Chris's wedding with me as my boyfriend, and I'll give him my parking spot in return."

Somewhere in the distance, a car alarm went off as her friends' mouths fell open. Retta watched them sit motionless for a while before Kym turned to Nia and asked, "I didn't hear that correctly, did I?"

Nia closed her mouth then opened it again. "Can you expand on this a little?"

After going into more detail, Retta said, "It's not really that big a deal."

"How's that not a big deal? You're faking an entire relationship," Kym said.

Retta huffed. "See, I was debating on not telling you because I knew you would judge—"

"Okay, okay," Nia said, lifting her hands. "Everyone relax. Take a breath." After a lengthy pause, Nia spoke, "He broke your heart, and you want to show you're doing better without him. I get it."

Sighing, Kym said, "It's wild how you're going about it, but if you need this wedding to close the chapter with Chris, I support you."

"Thank you."

"What's he like?" Nia asked.

Retta hesitated before saying, "Gorgeous. Tall and dark-skinned. Good sense of humor." She looked out the kitchen window, really visualizing Duncan now. "Thoughtful. He has this energy that makes you want to get closer."

It was in the way he carried himself—the tilt of his chin, the way he leveled his gaze at you when you spoke, and his forearms. He had incredible forearms.

"It sounds like you really like him," Nia said.

"Yeah, and how does this thing work? Are you two sleeping together?" Kym asked.

Straightening in her seat, Retta said, "It's one hundred percent professional…" She folded her hands in front of her on the counter. "But I did lick his face."

Nia laughed. "What? Why?"

"I thought he was going to kiss me. Then I realized it might be in my head. But it definitely looked like I was leaning in for a kiss, so I panicked and licked some frosting that was left from the cake eating contest we'd done."

"Well, this doesn't sound very professional," Kym said into her mug.

"Yeah, I might've messed things up. I have no idea if he wants to continue with this agreement. He might be too weirded out."

Her guard had dropped. She blamed the sugar high.

"Don't overthink it," Nia said. "Touch base and confirm that things are still going according to plan."

Retta let her friend's sensible words settle over her. "You're right."

Kym nodded. "Okay, but more on this cake eating contest."

———

Duncan's sister had joined him for one of his classes again, and he was now showing her all the advantages of having a sibling who owned a gym.

"Pressed juice, water, or kombucha?" Duncan asked, looking into the staff room refrigerator.

"Water," Gwen replied.

They stood near the table, and Duncan knew what his sister was about to ask before she said anything.

"So, have you started writing your speech?"

Duncan rubbed the back of his neck. "Kinda."

He'd not even thought about it yet.

"Let me guess. You've finished and are now going back to add iambic pentameter and make it rhyme," he said.

Gwen rolled her eyes. "Actually, I'm worried about it."

He frowned. "Why? Just string a few words together about the passage of time and happiness."

"See, that's exactly why I have to stress over it. I don't even know if you'll show up to the party let alone write a good speech."

Duncan shrugged. "I'll be there. I haven't decided if I want to commit to speaking though."

"That means there's more pressure on me to come up with something profound."

He sighed. Gwen had always been willing to add stress to her life to maintain harmony or make others happy. It was evident from her career path to her choice in boyfriends. "If I promise I'll write something, will you chill?"

She broke into a grin. "Yes."

"Fine."

"Good." Gwen punched his shoulder. "And thank you."

"Whatever," he said.

As Duncan was handing his sister some promotional

pens for her to take and share, Anthony burst through the staff room doors.

"What's taking you so long—" The big man skidded to a stop.

The hard planes of his business partner's face softened ever so slightly when he spotted Gwen.

"Hey, Tony," his sister said to Anthony.

Nobody in the entire world, that Duncan knew of, could get away with calling his best friend that. Ever since he'd known him, if anyone had slipped and shortened his name to Tony, he'd scowl and swiftly correct them. He assumed Anthony let it slide with Gwen simply on the strength of the two men's friendship.

"I didn't know you were coming in today," Anthony said, his eyes remaining steady on Gwen. "Is it your first class?"

"No, I was here a couple of weeks ago," she replied. "You guys have done an amazing job with this place."

"Thanks," Anthony said, smiling in a way that exposed his teeth.

Duncan frowned. The movement looked as unnatural as cracking plaster.

"I'll have to come in and try one of your classes," Gwen said.

"Yeah, for sure," Anthony replied, placing his hands on his hips. "Whenever you want to, let me know. Even if it's last minute, I'll put you on the schedule."

Gwen smiled. "I'll remember that."

A silence enveloped all three of them at that moment. Duncan cut through it by saying, "Okay, then, I'll walk you out."

———

The bakery had been closed for more than an hour, and Retta had spent most of that time watching a technician analyze and tinker with her water heater. Her landlord had finally sent someone over, and she was hoping the problem would be fixed with a twist of a bolt and a quick squirt of oil.

"Mhm… Interesting. Okay, I see."

She perked up, leaning over to see the man's progress. When professionals were doing their work, Retta preferred to give them space. However, this specific man had arrived and admitted that he didn't usually work with water heaters.

The technician finally emerged from the small room that held the apparatus and wiped his hands on a rag attached to his waist. "Well, you're right. There's a problem with your water heater."

Retta nodded and looked at him expectantly.

"I don't know what it is."

Her shoulders dropped. "So, where do we go from here?"

"I'll speak with my supervisor about bringing someone else up here to take a look."

"Okay, how long will that take?"

"A week or two. Maybe more."

Retta removed her glasses to relieve the pressure around the bridge of her nose. He gave her his card, and she thanked him before showing him out.

She quickly grabbed her bags, a basket of laundry, and locked up, not wanting to be in her store when the clamor started up again.

While she loaded her things into the back of her car, someone in the parking lot laughed. She knew who it belonged to, and a cursory glance over her shoulder confirmed that Duncan was standing there. It kind of disturbed her that she recognized his damn laugh already.

It had been several days since their date. She'd sent him her answers to the questionnaire, and he'd replied back with his and a smiley emoji. But other than that, she'd not interacted with him.

There was no way to gauge if the lack of communication was because they were in a fake relationship and conversations were strictly business, or if he was disengaging because he didn't know how to "break up" with her and maintain their new parking arrangement.

She needed to know either way.

As she approached the front entrance of the gym to wait, Duncan, by chance, turned and saw her. He stopped talking to the woman in front of him and shouted something that she didn't quite catch.

"I thought you'd be long gone by now," Duncan said once she closed the distance between them.

"I had a meeting with a technician for my water heater," Retta said.

"How did that go?"

She sighed. "It should be cleared up soon."

It looked like Duncan was going to ask her another question, but he must've remembered they weren't alone. "Retta, this is my sister, Gwen."

The woman looked like Duncan with her sharp cheekbones and dimpled smile. They shook hands.

Gwen looked between her and Duncan. "So, you are…"

"Neighbors," Retta said before Duncan could even open his mouth. "I own the bakery next door to the gym."

"Oh, I've been in there. I love the rhubarb galette."

"Thank you," Retta said.

Gwen smiled, and they exchanged a few more pleasantries before she hugged her brother and said, "I'm gonna head out. It was nice meeting you, Retta."

Once she'd driven off, Duncan fully turned to her. He stuffed his hands into his jacket's pockets.

"How've you been? I meant to text you," he said.

Oh, here it comes. They always started with the text they'd wanted to send.

"Are we still on for our second date?" he asked.

"Second date?" she squeaked.

"I was dead serious about watching *Rocky* with you. What kind of fake boyfriend would I be if I didn't introduce you to the best boxing movie of all time?"

Retta laughed, but her heart was beating rapidly. "Text me when you're free. We might have to do it during the week or for a few hours on the weekend."

"Perfect," he said. "I'll take care of the food."

Retta nodded. "I'd lick—like that."

Dammit.

His chuckle let her know he'd caught her Freudian slip, but buried under the heat of her embarrassment was relief he didn't hold the moment in the Uber against her.

Their conversation wound down, and they said goodbye.

She drove home lighter and happier, that was until she remembered their interactions were a means to an end. An end that would arrive in six weeks.

———

"Good morning," Duncan said, walking into the staff room for the monthly meeting with the other trainers.

He received a general rumbling response from the people already seated, and Anthony looked up from where he was fixing his morning shake.

Duncan smacked his friend on the back while he opened the fridge to place his lunch inside.

"We should get a bigger table," he said to Anthony as they leaned against the kitchenette counter, waiting for the rest of the team to arrive so they could begin the meeting. "Everyone should be able to sit at the table."

Anthony studied the furniture that already took up a lot of space. "Not in the budget."

"What's this?" a trainer they'd recently hired spoke loudly into the room.

She was studying the notice board where the team had placed Retta's Post-it notes. The ones where she in no uncertain terms told them to move their cars. They'd started collecting and displaying them on the board. Of course, it hadn't been added to in a while, and Duncan had forgotten all about it.

"Oh, man, for like a month some weirdo was leaving those notes on our cars," one trainer said. "We're keeping them as evidence in case one of us disappears."

Everyone laughed.

Without even a second thought, Duncan strode to the board and deftly removed the bright colored squares.

"Hey, what're you doing, boss?" someone asked.

He turned around to find his entire team watching him, including Anthony.

"Decluttering," he said as he transferred the paper to the waste bin.

They had all found the humor in the impassioned Post-it notes pleas, but it was ridiculous to make fun of them now. No one gave him a hard time. It was possible it was too early to give a shit about the end of a stale joke.

Returning to the counter where Anthony stood, Duncan ignored his friend's pointed stare.

"There's no need to mock people," Duncan explained.

"Right," Anthony replied. "We didn't really talk about your date."

Duncan took a drink of water from his bottle. "Fake date. And it was good. Informative."

If circumstances were different he'd probably be more effusive, but his friend was already skeptical about this setup. So, it wouldn't inspire confidence if Duncan went on about how he found Retta a surprising mix of awkward and bold.

At any given moment, he could see the gears turning in her head, but she did everything with gusto. He definitely didn't mention the superfluous second date. It was undoubtedly going against the hypothetical fake-dating manual he now felt compelled to write.

Anthony continued to study him. "You think you two are comfortable enough with each other now to make it believable?"

"Yeah, yeah," Duncan said, shrugging. She was definitely more comfortable with him. She licked his face, dammit.

"Why are you smiling?" Anthony asked.

"What? I can't smile now?"

His friend squinted.

"She's cool." Duncan could feel the eye-roll without even looking at his friend. He knew what he was thinking. "And no, I didn't sleep with her."

Not that he hadn't thought about it. It wasn't hard for him to envision Retta advancing upward from the foot of a bed where he lay. She wouldn't touch him until she got to his face where she'd lick him and whisper in his ear about wanting to taste more of him.

He blamed his unplanned months-long celibacy on all the dreams and thoughts. Another consequence of trying to get this business up and running. It was just his luck, however, that he'd start seeing someone who he had no intention of sleeping with. There were too many complicating factors for the possibility of an easy, no-strings-attached hook up.

That being said, he was operating under the understanding that getting involved with someone else right now would be some sort of a violation. So, jacking off in the shower would have to suffice for now.

Chapter Ten

RETTA HAD WOKEN up early and managed to run a few errands, clean her apartment, and start removing anything in her place that seemed even remotely romantic. For instance, the candles in her living room migrated to her bedroom, she didn't purchase flowers as she customarily did every other week, and she removed her doormat that read: "Love you, bye!"

Despite all the extra steps she was doing for Duncan's arrival, she'd insisted they do the movie watching at her place. This would allow her at least a bit of control. She needed a definitive end to this date seeing that during the last one, time had slipped by so quickly. There wouldn't be a midnight bedtime today. To ensure that even more, she'd scheduled this date on a night she was babysitting her brother's kids. Duncan had to be out of her apartment by four p.m.

At around noon, Retta was in the middle of making donuts she'd promised her niece and nephew when Duncan showed up to her apartment with a six-pack of beer, two different kinds of pizzas, and *Rocky* on DVD.

As he entered her home, a clean laundry smell accompanied him. The white t-shirt he wore looked great against his dark skin and seemed to accommodate his large frame so long as he didn't flex or stretch too much.

"I hope you're not loyal to a certain brand," he said, placing the beer on her counter.

"No," Retta said, averting her gaze from his arms.

"You making something?" he asked, pointing over her shoulder to the spot where her oil was heating.

"Yeah, I'm babysitting my niece and nephew in the evening. They both love chocolate donuts. I'm almost done here, then we can start the movie."

She resettled herself in front of the stove and proceeded to drop dough into the hot oil. The color darkened and a distinctive aroma bloomed.

"How can I help?" Duncan asked as he came to stand right behind her.

"You can wash your hands and chop the chocolate for the ganache," Retta said, gesturing toward the counter behind her.

"Knife?" he asked.

Retta turned and removed a knife from her butcher's block and handed it to him. She thought since he asked no further questions that he knew at least what he was doing, but then he started chopping the chocolate like you might a carrot.

After fishing her last donut from the oil, she turned to where he stood and gently pushed him to the side to demonstrate what she wanted him to do. Regaining control of the knife, he imitated her rough movements and completed the task.

"Okay, what next?" he asked, after popping a shard of chocolate into his mouth.

"Now, you have to heat the cream on the stove," she said, hauling out a pot from a low cupboard.

He opened her fridge and stepped back. "What the hell?"

"What?" she asked as she joined him to look inside her fridge. She expected to find her Jenga-like packed interior disrupted or something, but everything was perfectly in place.

"How can you find anything in here?" he asked.

Sure, there was a lot going on (stacked deli quart containers completely blocked the fridge's light), but there was intention behind the chaos.

"Where's the cream?" he asked.

"Okay, relax," Retta said as she started to move several of the perfectly labeled and dated containers onto the tiny counter beside them.

"There could be a live possum in there and you wouldn't know," Duncan said.

"His name is Terrance."

"What?" Duncan asked.

"The live possum in my refrigerator? His name is Terrance."

Duncan threw his head back and laughed. He didn't stop until Retta, after running out of counter space, started handing him jars and bottles to hold.

After finding the carton and returning the other items, they got the ganache going.

"You have to watch it. Don't look away for anything," Retta said of the cream in the pot. "You want to take it off just before it's about to boil."

Duncan folded his arms and while staring at the cream asked, "What's the weirdest event you've catered for?"

Retta paused with the dishes she was cleaning,

pondering the question. "I don't think there's been anything completely weird. I did do this wedding held at a pool with a couple that wore mermaid tails during the ceremony."

"You're kidding."

"No, it was unique, and everyone was fully invested in the theme," Retta said.

They didn't delve deeper into the topic of weird and wonderful events because she pointed to the scalded cream and said, "It's done, remove it and pour it over the chocolate in the bowl."

After a minute, she had him whisk the ingredients together as she got two cooled donuts from the rack.

"This doesn't look right," Duncan said of the clumpy mess of cream and chocolate.

"It'll come together. Keep going."

He whisked and whisked, and eventually a silky ganache appeared.

"See, told you," she said, dipping their donuts in and holding them up for Duncan to inspect.

Taking one from her hand, he bit into more than half of it.

"This is incredible," he said.

She beamed. "If I was making it only for us, I would've used a little more dark chocolate and maybe some espresso, but kids aren't usually fans of the bitter note."

"Okay, I need to step away from these," Duncan said, finishing off his donut. "I thought after the cake eating contest I was done with sweets for at least a month, but here I am." He moved out of the kitchen into the living room. "You want to start the movie?"

"Yeah," she said as she caught her reflection in a small mirror above the table where she kept her keys and mail. She looked exactly like you might expect someone who'd spent all morning doing work and running errands.

"You can start the movie, I'll be right back," Retta said as she sped walked to her bedroom.

She quickly fixed her hair, blotted her face, and threw her apron into the clothes hamper before leaving her bedroom. As she approached the living area she said, "I have this amazing blood orange caramel sauce that would also go well with the donu—"

Retta stopped short of entering the room. She found Duncan studying the paused TV screen. There couldn't have been a worse thing for her to forget in the DVD player. The video was frozen on an image of her from a few years ago. Happy tears streamed down her face as she held a recognizable trophy in her hands.

He turned to her. "You won *Winner Bakes All?*"

There were several ways she usually answered this question. The goal was to get out of the conversation as fast as possible, but she'd been caught off guard today.

"Yeah," Retta finally replied, moving to the DVD player to remove the disc and add the *Rocky* one.

Every once in a while, when she was alone and wanted to wallow in self-pity, and was definitely on her period, she'd watch herself win one of the biggest baking competition shows.

"That's amazing," Duncan said. "I once spent a whole weekend binge-watching it."

Maybe he gained a little bit more respect for her and her work. But like many times before, she'd have to watch the awe morph into some version of pity.

"Except nobody has any idea I won," she said.

Duncan frowned. "That show is huge though."

Retta grabbed a beer and a couple slices of pizza and settled into her armchair. "You know Pierre Gustov?"

"The judge with the little…" Duncan waved his hand above his head to demonstrate Gustov's signature hairstyle.

"Yeah, well, he was indicted for fraud a month before the premiere of my season."

Retta, bright-eyed and new to the professional baking world, had submitted her casting video on a whim. She'd put it out of her mind and hadn't told anyone she'd applied. So, when she'd received a call from the producers of the show telling her they wanted her to move ahead in the audition process, she was absolutely shocked.

"But wait, how did his crime affect you?" he asked.

"Oh, they pulled the entire season."

There was silence as Duncan's face moved in all sorts of directions. "What do you mean they pulled the entire season?"

"Just that. They stopped running ads for it, and the episodes never aired on TV. My win was mentioned on their website, and they uploaded a ninety-second clip of me actually winning the season on their Facebook page."

"Retta—"

"Meanwhile, I'd been promoting the fact I was a contestant for weeks. There were viewing parties already scheduled."

She forced herself to stop talking. He didn't need to know all the details. But looking up at Duncan for the first time since she'd started rambling, she was taken aback by how upset he looked.

"I'm so sorry," he said.

"Thanks." She got up from her spot to grab the remote and draw the blinds to eliminate the glare on the television. "Enough about that. Let's get ready to rumble."

Duncan finally cracked a smile, and Retta returned to her seat and spent the first five minutes of the movie replaying the previous moments. The story eventually drew her in, but somewhere along the way she fell asleep.

———

Duncan, for the first time in the dozenth viewing of this film, was distracted and not at all interested in Rocky Balboa's journey.

He'd spent a lot of the time on his phone, looking for remnants of Retta's win on the internet. This deep dive was possible because she'd fallen asleep thirty minutes into the movie.

There were a few articles here, a write up there, but nothing like he could find on previous winners. There was a clear trajectory for all champions of *Winner Bakes All*. Tiffany Fletcher was a bestselling cookbook author. Michael Aayomi had his own network TV show. Sara Cleaver was a personal pastry chef to the freakin Prime Minister.

After he'd finished reading all he could read about her win, he stewed over the unfairness of the whole situation. When the movie end credits rolled, the room was left in darkness. He remained seated and made no move to wake up Retta, but she did anyway minutes later. Her hair was in its natural curly state fastened into a puff, and it had shifted off-center while she'd slept.

"How long have I been out?" she asked, unfolding her body from the armchair.

"The movie is done," he said, watching her silhouette as she leisurely raised her hands above her head.

She snorted. "Well, damn. I'm sorry."

"It's fine," he said before coughing to clear the gruffness from his voice.

"I didn't fall asleep because I thought it was boring. The fifteen minutes I saw? Perfection," she said, picking up the dirty plates from the coffee table.

As she walked into the kitchen, he was still so caught

up in his thoughts that he didn't hear Retta's question until she asked it for the second time. "Do you want a donut to go—"

"Did you get the prize money?"

She paused and studied him. "Are you still thinking about that?"

"You deserved that money. You deserved that moment in the sun."

"I don't know," she said, laughing a bit. "I've always really enjoyed rainy days."

Duncan didn't react to her attempt at a joke, and she pushed up her glasses with her knuckles and sighed.

"I got my prize money and paid off a bunch of debt from school and opened Dutch."

The tension around his neck and shoulders eased a bit. "Good." He still wished that she could've seen more success.

"Do you want that donut now?" she asked, moving through the kitchen. She opened a cabinet and even with her height failed to reach the Tupperware stored on the top shelf. Before he could offer to get it for her, she hoisted herself up on her counter.

Automatically, he was behind her posed to catch her if she made the wrong move. "Careful."

"I'm fine," she said, twisting to grab the containers she desired.

When she returned to the ground, they were standing close to each other. So much so, he caught the subtle fragrance she wore. He wondered where she applied it. Her wrists? The back of her neck? Maybe between her breasts.

Her eyes widened as she looked at him in his face. "A-also, you can take the rest of the pizza. You saw my fridge. I have no space."

"You should get a step stool," he said.

"I know."

This was the moment she'd make a move to the counter with the donuts or he'd step out of her way, but they both remained planted in their spots. The longer they stood there, the more details he took note of—like the rise and fall of her chest and the way she stared at his mouth.

Duncan took a shallow breath. "If you keep looking at me like that, we're gonna be in trouble, and we don't want that."

There was a beat of silence before she looked in his eyes and asked, "No?"

And that was it.

He descended on her lips like they were his source of life. They were warm and soft and perfectly fit against his. Dropping the containers in her hands, she wrapped her arms around his neck, pulling him further into her body. Her tongue, delicate and polite at first, stoked a fire in him, and he cupped either side of her face, trying to preserve the tenderness that wanted to fade in favor of an urgent forcefulness. But his efforts proved futile the second she moaned into his mouth.

———

Everything in Retta's body was operating in service of Duncan's touch. She hadn't meant for this date to unfold this way, but while she was here, maybe she could indulge a little. His lips were demanding and hot.

Every time his tongue met hers, heat would unfurl and she'd press herself closer to him. The grip he had on her hips was almost painful, and her breaths were coming in the moments when he'd break their kiss to run his lips against her jaw or neck.

Her hands skimmed his body as she tried to find the best place to settle them. But she was convinced the man wasn't made of flesh but of warm marble. When she finally slipped her hand underneath his shirt, the muscles she found there twitched under her touch.

It didn't seem like they could get any closer until Duncan grabbed her thigh and drew her to him. The bulge in the front of his pants pressed against her lower stomach. A thrum reverberated across her body, and she didn't recognize they were moving until the cool edge of her kitchen counter touched her back.

Before he could lift her onto the surface she said, "Not near the food. Not near the food."

She pushed him toward the living room, and along the way both their shirts came off. When he fell backward onto the couch, she didn't hesitate before straddling him. The way her legs were spread, heightened her need, and she pressed herself against Duncan's thigh to relieve the pressure.

Low moans followed as she slowly moved herself up and down his hard thigh. Warmth and sparks flooded her body.

"Is this how you'd ride my face?" he whispered against her ear as he grabbed her hips in that unforgiving hold.

The thought of his tongue and mouth against her made her increase the pressure and quicken her pace.

"That's it. Take what you need," he said.

She wanted to respond to the alluring timbre of his voice by breathing his name, but she bit her lip instead and continued swiveling against the slabs of muscle underneath her.

He ran kisses down her neck and bare shoulders before unfastening her bra. "Fuck," he said, squeezing her exposed breasts.

"Harder."

He responded by giving her pert nipples a pinch. The spark of pain directly shot to her clit, and she grabbed his shoulder to stabilize herself.

"I swear to God, if you come from just this…" he said, cutting himself off to take a nipple into his mouth.

Reaching down, she touched the front of his pants, but before she could explore or tease him, the distinct buzz of her phone caught her attention.

She froze.

"What's up?" Duncan asked, pulling away.

Reaching for her cell phone on the side table, she read the message on the screen. "Shit." Covering her breasts with her arm, Retta got up from Duncan's lap. "They're on their way."

Her brother and his kids would arrive thirty minutes before she'd expected them. She turned on all the living room lights, and Duncan tossed her bra. He picked up his beer bottle and returned the coasters before straightening the shifted books on the coffee table.

Once her bra and shirt were on, Retta opened the blinds and placed the throw pillows back on the sofa. She escaped to the bathroom and washed her hands and made sure she didn't look like she'd been doing what she'd been doing. God, her intention had simply been to make out with the man.

When she returned to the living area, Duncan was wearing his t-shirt once again and the kitchen counters were clear of the pizza boxes and bottles. There was no sign that he'd stepped foot in the apartment. Well, except the fact that he was still in her home.

"We probably shouldn't do that again, right?" she said, laughing awkwardly and avoiding eye contact.

He smiled, rubbing the back of his neck.

"Not because it wasn't good," she quickly added. "I was close to…"

"Coming? Yeah, I could sense that."

"I'm sure it would've been great, but maybe it's for the best it didn't happen because once you see someone's orgasm face it's hard to *turn back time.*"

Duncan tilted his head. "What's that sound you made?"

"Sorry, that was my Cher impression. I don't know why I did that… What I'm trying to say is this is a unique situation and we don't want to muddy the waters."

She was already unsettled about her attraction to him, adding sex wouldn't help.

He nodded. "I agree."

"Good," she said, fidgeting with her glasses. "You should probably go before—"

The apartment door buzzed.

"I guess you're meeting more people from my life," Retta said as she pressed the button to grant entrance into the apartment complex.

"It went well the first time. Also, your shirt's on backward," he said.

She quickly corrected it and soon after heard the excited pitter-patter of her niece and nephew running down the hall. The moment she opened the door, Alicia and Emmanuel ran for the kitchen to find the treats she'd promised them over the phone.

"Hi, Auntie," they both said in unison before disappearing behind the counter.

"Sorry," her brother, Kevin, said. "Tabitha needs to pick some stuff from her mother's before we—"

Kevin stopped when he spotted Duncan casually standing beside her.

"Who's that?" Alicia asked with her mouth full.

"Ah, this is Duncan."

Her brother's eyebrows raised in question, before settling into a neutral plane. "Nice to meet you."

The men exchanged handshakes before Duncan went over to her niece and nephew and similarly gave each of them a handshake.

"The chocolate is pretty good, right?" Duncan asked, getting down to their level.

The two kids nodded, ganache already all over their mouths and chins. All three of them proceeded to chat about their favorite chocolate desserts.

"How long?" her brother asked softly as he handed her two small backpacks.

Retta shrugged. "It's new," she said, vaguely.

Her brother nodded. "I'm happy for you."

A pang of guilt hit her. She wished he had something real to be happy for her about.

"Well, sorry for interrupting you this afternoon," Kevin said.

"No problem. I have to head out anyway," Duncan said, standing up and joining them near the door.

Her brother looked at his kids. "Be good for Auntie. I love you."

They were already preoccupied and detached from whatever their father was saying.

"Hold on, I'll walk down with you," Duncan said to her brother.

For some reason, them leaving her place at the same time made her nervous, but she didn't have the chance to overthink that because both men quickly left her apartment. Turning to her wards for the evening, Retta put on her brightest smile. She'd have to throw herself into this task to not reflect on how this relationship was progressing.

Chapter Eleven

DUNCAN FOUND himself pacing his small office during a short break one afternoon. He was expanding on the few bullet points he'd made for the speech he'd read at his parent's divorce party. Or at least he was trying to. But if he was honest, he was finding the process more difficult than he'd expected. Everything he wrote sounded sappy.

Sure, he could lean into the sentiment, but that would require parsing out his feelings about the most turbulent relationship he'd ever had the displeasure of witnessing.

As he was googling yet another synonym for "great", Anthony entered the room and moved to the shelf in the corner where they stored office supplies.

"I thought you went out for lunch."

"No, I'm working on my speech," Duncan said, sighing.

His friend looked up from where he was refilling a stapler. "For the divorce party? You've decided to go?"

Duncan rubbed his face. "Yeah. Mostly because Gwen is going and making a speech. I can't leave her hanging."

"How's"—his friend cleared his throat—"Gwen handling everything?"

"Oh, she's being Gwen, meticulous and keen."

Anthony smiled before he straightened his features and asked, "What do you have written so far?"

"What?"

"Your speech. Read it," Anthony said as he moved to sit on the edge of the table that Duncan wasn't so sure would hold the man's weight.

"It's nothing special."

"I have five minutes till my next class," Anthony said.

Seeing his friend was dead serious about him sharing his words, Duncan looked down at his phone and read, "'Good afternoon, distinguished guests. I thought I'd be sadder than I am today. My parents are getting a divorce, after all, but I'm excited for them. They are loving amazing parents, and I hope they get to live exciting and fulfilling lives separately.'" Duncan looked up at his friend. "This is where I'd go into a story or a childhood memory of some kind. I'm not sure yet."

Anthony was studying him closely, and Duncan braced himself for his critique.

"What's the point you're trying to make with this speech?" Anthony asked.

"I'm not trying to make a point. I'm trying to say enough to fill up five minutes. That's it."

"Then it's perfect," Anthony said.

There was no judgment in his tone, but Duncan felt he needed to add, "I'm nervous they're using this party to stall what needs to be done. They've threatened divorce so many times before, and it never happened."

Granted this was the furthest his parents had made it in the process, but the possibility of them not going through with it was still there. Their waffling was one of the reasons why relationships were terrifying to Duncan. Disharmony could become comfortable.

"I don't want to put all this work into a bunch of words I might not ever read out loud," Duncan said.

"Then don't," Anthony said, standing up.

That type of comment made by anyone else would sound insincere and flippant, but it was the type of straightforward advice Anthony doled out. He tried to live an uncomplicated life and saw many things as black and white.

"However you approach this speech, I hope you realize it won't change how things unfold with your folks. They're going to do what they're going to do."

Duncan nodded, dropping into the chair behind his desk. If only *thinking* about the feelings surrounding his parent's divorce had him feeling like he'd gone several rounds with a formidable opponent, there was no way he was opening that can of worms, especially in front of an audience.

"Is Retta going with you to the party?"

Duncan straightened in his seat. "Why would you ask that?"

"I don't know, since you have regularly scheduled dates now."

He'd accidentally let it slip that he'd been at Retta's apartment for a movie. "There's no reason for her to come to the party," Duncan said.

Except maybe that she'd make it patently more enjoyable with her enthusiasm and sense of humor that matched his own.

"And it wasn't a real date," Duncan added. "It was a public service. She'd never watched *Rocky*."

His statements might've sounded less odd to his own ears if he hadn't been torturing himself for days thinking about Retta sitting on his lap, making lustful sounds that echoed in his head during his morning jack off sessions.

"As long as you can still tell the difference," Anthony said.

"Of course I can."

Their lives were getting entangled in ways that were foreign to Duncan. He'd met maybe one of his ex's siblings. But he was grateful Retta had been clearheaded enough to insist they keep at least one aspect of their arrangement straightforward.

Anthony crossed his arms. "You—"

"Aren't your five minutes up already?"

———

Whether because of strong coffee or the anticipation for upcoming presentations, the people in the hotel conference room Retta stood in chatted excitedly. She adjusted the platters of pastries she had delivered and took a photo for social media. Having already spoken with the programmer for the business event, she picked up her belongings to take her leave.

"Excuse me," Retta said as she navigated her way around men in gray suits toward the exit. When swinging the door open, she almost crashed into a person who was trying to enter at the same time.

"I'm sorry—"

Retta's eyes widened when she finally straightened and looked into the man's face.

"Hi," she said automatically, already hating herself for speaking. She usually didn't make it a habit of acknowledging men who ghosted her.

Steve looked unchanged from the time of their first

date at the cafe, except he was in a boring suit like the other men in the hall.

"Ah, hey… This is awkward," Steve said, laughing and sweeping his floppy brown hair to the side.

Oh, please. That was on him. He was the one who hadn't responded to her texts.

"Not really," Retta replied.

Steve's lips turned downward, but he didn't say anything. So, she nodded and moved to sidestep him.

"Can I ask you something?"

God, what now?

"I thought we had a great time. What happened?" he asked, fidgeting with his briefcase.

Retta shook her head. "What are you talking about? I texted you once our date ended and two more times the day after."

He'd given her his number and told her to text him so he got hers as well.

Steve stepped forward, frowning. "I didn't receive one message from you."

They stood there, staring each other down. Retta was trying to gauge if this man was bullshitting her or not, a quick bait and switch because now he wanted a chance with her but knew he'd already messed up.

"You must've typed my number incorrectly," he said.

Sure, I did.

Retta resisted rolling her eyes as she retrieved her phone from her pocket and pulled up his contact information still programmed in. Holding up the device, she waited for him to verify his number.

"The second two is supposed to be a three," he said, looking up from the screen.

"Crap," she said, bringing the phone back to her face

to study the sequence of numbers. "I thought you ghosted me."

He smiled. "Me, too."

They both laughed. Well, a piece of her ego had been restored, and for the little she'd thought of him in the intervening weeks, she was happy his good character had been returned as well.

"I'm glad we got to clear that one up," she said.

"Yeah, I really did enjoy our date."

She smiled and nodded. "That story you told me about the gorilla reserve you went to in Rwanda stuck with me."

He laughed and pulled a face that he did to demonstrate his fear at being so close to the magnificent beasts.

Her attention was momentarily drawn to the voice in the conference room letting attendees know that the opening remarks would begin in a few minutes.

When she turned back to Steve to tell him goodbye, he said, "I'd like to go out with you again."

Now, *this* was awkward.

"Oh, that's sweet," she said, internally cringing at how condescending the comment sounded. She might as well have included a pat on his head. "Unfortunately, I'm seeing someone right now."

While technically not true, the lie slid from her easily. It was too late to back out now from her arrangement with Duncan. He had her scone recipe for God's sake.

Steve softly smiled. "Understandable. You're a catch, but if anything changes…" He handed her his card with his correct cell number on it and walked into the large room.

———

It was the end of the day, and Retta was ready to get home. However, the team was talking amongst themselves and were in no rush to leave.

"What are you waiting for? Go enjoy your evening," Retta said as she finished up the last part of her shutdown routine.

"Ah, I wish," Omar said. "But Philippa is dragging us next door for a workout."

Laughing, Retta looked between the three of them. "Why?"

"She has a little crush on one of the trainers next door," Cheyenne said.

Retta stilled. "Who?"

It felt like an eternity waiting for Cheyenne to respond with, "The redhead, Trevor."

Retta relaxed her grip on the counter and smiled. "Is that where you've been disappearing off to for lunch the past week?"

Everyone turned to Philippa with smirks.

"I have no idea what you're talking about," she replied as she opened her front-facing camera to smooth down her hair.

"Ok, sure," Retta said, laughing. "Well, have fun—"

"You should come with us," Omar said.

Retta made protesting sounds.

"Yeah, it can be part of our team building or whatever you force us to do each summer," Philippa said.

"I thought you all enjoyed those," Retta said, frowning.

Omar nudged Philippa with his elbow before saying, "We do. That's why you should come."

"You also get a discount since you work in the complex," Cheyenne said.

Retta wished she could say she agreed to go because she wanted to get a workout in, but in all honesty, she kind of wanted to have the chance to see Duncan after their date several days ago. Why had she so definitively shut down the possibility of sex like she regularly made insightful and mature decisions? Once, an infomercial convinced her to buy two car French fry holders.

"I think I have some clothes in my trunk that could work," Retta said.

But it turned out that the workout gear she kept in her car on the off chance she'd feel like working out after a day at the bakery had been raided. It had probably happened during a time she'd spilled something on herself and needed a change of clothes.

What remained was a flimsy sports bra and spandex pants she was sixty percent sure were not opaque.

Entering Spotlight Boxing with her bakery branded t-shirt, she stood at the front counter as her team checked in.

When it was her turn, the young woman behind the desk smiled and looked down at her tablet before asking, "Hi, your name?"

"Oh, I haven't registered, I was hoping to drop in for the class."

The woman made a single tsk. "Unfortunately, we're completely full for the six o'clock class, but if you want, we can fit you in for the seven-thirty bootcamp?"

Retta shook her head. "No, that's okay." She turned to her employees. "There's no space. I think I'll head home."

"Are you sure?" Philippa asked the woman behind the counter.

"It's fine. Next time we'll plan better. Have fun, okay?" Retta said. Though she was disappointed, she was also a bit grateful she wouldn't have to experience to what extent her sports bra was unsuitable for boxing.

But as that thought crossed her mind, Duncan rounded the corner. She'd literally come to the gym expecting to catch a glimpse of him, but nevertheless her stomach flipped when she spotted him.

When he saw her, he stopped dead in his tracks despite walking and talking with someone else. Their eyes met, and he smiled at her before regarding her from head to toe. Every nerve ending in her body fired off as she looked away to temper down suspicion from her team. She didn't want to answer questions the following day.

"Bakers night out?" Duncan asked as he came to stand next to her.

The side of his body brushed up against hers, and it took everything in her not to react like she'd touched a hot plate.

"Yeah, thought we should take advantage of such a reputable place," Omar said.

With his dimple on full display, Duncan said, "Smart. You're here for the six o'clock class?"

They nodded.

"You'll enjoy it. Trevor is a great trainer."

Philippa perked up at the mention of Trevor's name. It was the first time she stopped methodically scanning the foyer for signs of him.

"Well, since it's your first class here, and I have a bit of time, I can show you how to wrap your hands. You'll be ready to go," he said.

"I'm actually not joining them today," Retta said as her team members all revealed the wraps they'd been given.

Duncan turned his gaze on her. "Why not?"

"I didn't book ahead of time," she explained.

He nodded and walked over to the front desk.

"Oh, he's about to hook you up," Philippa whispered as they watched Duncan talk to the woman behind the counter.

"You're in," Duncan said, rejoining the group. "We typically see one to two no-shows, so it should be fine."

Retta's heart soared, but not because she was going to get to work out with her crew.

"Okay, let's get this hand wrapping tutorial started," Duncan said, moving them off to the side, away from the door and welcoming mat.

For the entire demonstration, he spoke confidently and repeated where it was needed. After checking each person's final product, Duncan gave them the go-ahead to make their way down to the gym. Retta was the last one he approached.

"How's it going?" he asked, almost whispering the question.

She pressed her glasses firmly on her face. "I think they're okay." She offered her hands for inspection.

"This one's too tight," he said, narrowing the distance between their bodies. "You'll lose feeling."

She clumsily unraveled the wrap before he took hold of her freed arm. As he slowly moved the material around her hand, she became aware of her own heartbeat. It was loud and persistent, and the longer they stood there, the more restless she became.

"Don't mind the calluses," she said in hopes of distracting him from the rapid pulse in her wrist.

Flipping her hand so her palm faced upwards, Duncan studied the rough patches where her digits and palm met. He gently ran his thumb over them.

"What are they from?" he asked, resuming his hand wrapping.

"Work," she explained.

His eyebrows raised. "Baking?"

People thought bakers pranced through icing sugar and

worked to the sound of chirping birds, but rolling dough with a hard pin for hours on end was no joke.

"Yeah, they used to be worse when I worked in a commercial kitchen during my apprenticeship."

"That's kinda badass."

A few moments later, he'd completed his task and said, "You're good to go." But his hand remained around her fingertips.

"Thanks," she said, her beating heart flaring once again.

It took several more seconds for him to finally release her, and as they walked down the hallway together, the chatter of the class downstairs grew louder. But all Retta could focus on were the tiny sparks that would skate over her skin every time some part of her body grazed Duncan's. Was he feeling them too? Did he think about the day at her apartment at regular intervals like she'd been doing?

When they reached the top of the stairs and ramp that took people down to the gymnasium, she turned to say goodbye and found him looking at her with such intensity. His hands clenched and unclenched, and neither of them said anything. The tingling that had been isolated to her arm now ran rampant across her entire body. It wasn't clear who moved first, but it didn't matter once they were embracing and their lips were touching.

They were on the move, but she wasn't exactly sure where to. His strong arms encircled her waist, and while stumbling and careening backward to an unknown destination, she never worried they'd hit a wall or fall. He tasted faintly of spearmint, and she could feel the stubble on his face he usually kept shaven.

Eventually, they entered a room where the door muted the noise on the other side. It was here where she heard their erratic breathing and truly felt her body's response to the man before her.

————

Duncan hadn't expected to see Retta today, and he might've let her go off to her class if she hadn't turned around and looked at him with her big brown eyes stark with desire. He'd abandoned his commitment to keeping things straightforward the moment he saw it.

She was kissing him and running her hands down his bare arms, and he could barely make sense of anything. His brain told him to get her on some sort of surface. He moved them toward a table and swept his arm across it. Papers, pens, and a full mug of cold coffee hit the floor.

Her breath hitched when he picked her up and placed her on the edge of the desk.

Not wasting any time, he spread her legs wide and settled in between them. Kissing her deeply, his body flooded with heat when she grabbed the back of his neck and pressed closer to him.

"I've been thinking about this," Retta said against his mouth.

"About what?" he asked.

"You touching me."

He found it difficult to breathe for a moment. "How? When? When do you think about that?"

Running his lips against her neck where her rapid pulse danced underneath her skin, he waited for an answer. But the sound of someone walking past the door distracted her.

Moving her chin so she'd look at him, he said, "The door is locked. No one's getting in."

She nodded and slipped her hand underneath his shirt, her fingers skimming across his abs and chest. He gritted his teeth, and managed to ask again, "When do you think about me touching you?"

"Every time—" She removed her hands from his body and pushed up her t-shirt, tugging the thin sports bra down until her chest was exposed. "I'm trying to fall asleep or get myself off to relieve stress."

He exhaled roughly and studied the way her breasts jutted out as an offering. Perfect. They were absolutely perfect. Round and small enough to comfortably fit in his palms.

"Stressed about?" he asked, mostly because he didn't like the idea of her being stressed.

She released a breathy laugh. "Money, the bakery, climate change—"

Her words were cut short when she whimpered as he lightly ran his thumb over her stiffened brown nipple.

"You're so sensitive."

"I know," she replied as her words turned into a throaty moan when he took one of her hard nipples into his mouth.

In response, she grabbed the back of his head. He needed to grow out his hair a bit, he decided then. Feeling her grip tighten around his coils would be his priority. She arched her back, and he felt more than heard the carnal sounds escaping her lips.

He pressed his knuckles against her clit over her pants and made lazy circles, carefully watching her until he got the right rhythm and speed that had her breathing shallow and her eyes half open. Grabbing his hardening dick, he willed it to work with him at this time.

When Retta released another moan, this one a little more unbridled, he asked, "Do you want everyone to hear us? Is that your thing?"

She shook her head, delirious as she pressed the back of her wrapped hand against her mouth.

Watching the woman who was a fucking wet dream incarnate try to hold in her ecstasy was doing something to him.

While kissing the space between her breasts, he worked to pull her pants off her soft thighs.

Once bare on the table, he took a second to study her. Nipples slick from his tongue, red panties, and legs spread wide.

Her eyes were on him as he bent low and brushed his lips against her stomach before journeying down her leg.

He kissed her inner thigh, relishing the warmth of her skin. Determined to go slow, he lightly ran his fingers over the damp material that hid her pussy from his sight. However, her responsive inhale and attempts to scoot closer almost had him ripping the delicate fabric. He needed to get his mouth on her.

Hooking his fingers under the waistband, he moved to tug them off in one fell swoop, but a knock sounded at the door. "Duncan?"

Retta sat up so fast, almost taking out his head as she swung to close her legs and stand.

Duncan straightened from his stooped position, trying to get his heartbeat to level off and his dick to go down.

"Yup?" he called out, hoping his voice didn't sound strained.

"Are you busy? I need to run over some things with you," the person, one of the trainers, behind the door said.

He closed his eyes and swallowed the shout he wanted to release. "I'll meet you in the staff room."

Once the footsteps retreated, he turned to Retta who was already straightening her clothes.

"It's a sign," she whispered, hurriedly pulling up her pants. "We should stop trying to do this."

He'd been sure not sleeping with her was a good idea, but things changed when clothes came off.

"Screw rules and hypothetical fake-dating manuals," he said.

"Huh?"

Duncan came around to where she sat on the edge of the table, trampling on the documents strewn on the ground. He placed his hands on the desk on either side of her and said, "Who are we fooling?"

She frowned. "M-my family?"

"No, what I mean is we're ridiculous for thinking this isn't going to happen." He leaned in close. "I want it. That pretty pussy of yours wants it. And when it happens, we'll go slow and be as loud as we want."

He watched her chest rise and fall, and he wasn't sure how she'd respond.

"I look forward to it, then," she said, kissing him and walking out the door.

Chapter Twelve

RETTA SAT on the plush ottoman in a department store, watching Nia rapidly rifle through clothing racks. Her stylish friend would only pause long enough to pull out an item and study it before either returning it or throwing the clothing over her arm.

"Any day now, girl," Kym said from her place next to Retta on the wide seat.

Nia looked at Kym. "Do you want her to look great or not?"

Kym lifted her hands in surrender, and their friend resumed her search. Retta solicited the most fashionable person she knew to find outfits for the engagement party as well as the wedding.

This errand wasn't completely necessary, because Retta had a couple appropriate pieces in her closet. But they were the two outfits she wore to every fancy function. As a result, she'd worn both of them several times throughout her years with Chris, from office holiday parties to dinner with his parents. There was even photographic evidence.

If she was going through all the trouble to fake a relationship to attend her ex-boyfriend's wedding, shouldn't she fully commit to making a statement? To Retta that meant not showing up in a predictable dress her ex-boyfriend helped her into once upon a time.

"Okay," Nia said, coming over to where the two women sat. Both of her arms were draped with dresses.

"This side is more conservative and elegant," Nia said, raising her left arm. "These dresses will make people sit up straight and shut the hell up."

Nia's intensity and care for this process was inspiring, but Retta was still a little overwhelmed with the number of choices.

"My vote is for the right side," Kym said.

"Let me try some on, and we can see," Retta said, taking two dresses, one from each pile, into the change room.

She tried the more conventional dress on first, liking the flowy fabric and the fact that she could eat without any fussy, tight material constricting her.

She exited the change room and Kym instantly said, "No, ma'am."

"What?" Retta asked, touching the dress and twirling around to look at herself in the full-length mirror. "I like it."

Nia approached and pulled the garment to get it to sit better around Retta's bust.

"You look like a Reverend's wife. Or a woman who still has a landline," Kym said.

Retta frowned at her friend.

Nia scoffed and said, "Girl, shut up. There's nothing wrong with a Reverend's wife or landlines, and I think this is a very nice option. It's sophisticated. There's some interesting construction in the neckline, and it's perfectly suitable for a church wedding."

Retta tilted her head.

"What do you think?" Nia coaxed. "How do you *feel* in it?"

"It's fine," she replied. But that's just it, fine would not do.

She returned to the change room, taking more dresses with her. However, this time all of them were from the hot pile. When she emerged wearing one of the sexy dresses, it wasn't a great fit for her tall body. The next one made her already wide shoulders more prominent; she felt like a linebacker.

But she eventually stepped into a luxe emerald green A-line dress that hit her mid-thigh. It sat off the shoulder and almost looked like a lopsided bow.

She loved it.

"This one for the wedding," Retta said.

Nodding, Nia said, "I agree. And then you can wear the black slinky one for the engagement party."

Kym stood up, rubbing her lower back. "I know you two aren't actually a couple, but Duncan is going to die when he sees you in the black one."

The hairs on Retta's arms stood up at the thought of Duncan narrowing his eyes and looking at her with a maddening half smile. It would reveal a whisper of the dimple in his cheek.

She shook her head. Who knew getting yanked from the precipice of an orgasm made you wax-poetic?

"How's the arrangement between you two going anyway?" Nia asked.

Retta's mind went immediately to the moment when Duncan was between her thighs. "Good. No complaints."

However, she was a little uncomfortable with how much she'd revealed to him on that table. Not because they weren't true or she was ashamed of her desires, but because there was some control she relinquished when she admitted how much she wanted him.

They were no longer operating under the guise that everything they did was strategic and artificial. But perhaps it was okay to allow herself to get swept up in her attraction to Duncan. When the curtains dropped and their arrangement was over, none of it would be held against her.

Kym, unaware of Retta's thoughts, said, "Great. So, now you have a beautiful dress, a fine ass date, and you're ready to make a scene at these wedding events."

———

Teetering in shoes Nia suggested she wear, Retta arrived at a condo where Chris and Irene's engagement party was being held. She'd intended to arrive earlier but had gotten lost. A small part of her hoped she'd fail to find the place, so she could be free to return home and eat pie from the tin and watch reruns of home-reno shows. But no such luck.

As she rode the elevator to the thirty-third floor with a macaron tower in her hands, she reminded herself why she was doing this. Once in front of the correct door, she barely touched it before it swung open to reveal the interior of the home. A dozen or so enthusiastic guests she didn't recognize were already mingling. They talked with their hands and laughed loudly like they discovered they'd all gone to the same high school. There was no sign of Duncan, however.

"Retta," someone called out.

Irene's mother smiled and made quick work toward her.

"Hi, Auntie," Retta said to the older woman after bracing herself for the interaction.

"Come in, please," her Aunt Wendy said. She led Retta farther into the luxury condo and kept looking behind as if to make sure she was still following.

When they arrived in the kitchen, Retta carefully placed the creation on the counter next to the other desserts.

"This is beautiful," her aunt said as she pulled out her phone to take a picture.

"I'm glad you like it."

Retta took her aunt's momentary distraction to look around. Two tables that could easily fit fifty guests, were set in the middle of the room she stood in. The enormous windows to her left provided a beautiful view of the city and brought in the setting sun's golden light. Beyond the immediate space before her, she spotted a living room that had been turned into a dance floor for the occasion.

"All right, my dear, I have to take care of some things, but I'll find you tonight so we can catch up a little more," Aunt Wendy said as she offered a hug.

After picking up a cocktail from the bar, Retta slinked closer to where the other guests were congregating. She couldn't have felt more out of place if she were playing maracas and doing an Irish jig.

More people arrived, and she smiled at those she'd met when she was with Chris. None of them maintained eye contact with her. She didn't hold it against them, however, because Retta knew her own friends wouldn't be quick to make conversation with one of her exes. Consequently, she was left to study the artwork on the walls as she waited for at least one of her many cousins or Duncan to show up.

During her turn around the room, a coldness settled over her as she noticed one specific detail. The archway made of balloons, the floral centerpieces on the tables, and the elaborate signage near the dance floor were all purple.

Not just any purple either. This particular shade was one Retta knew intimately because she'd spent weeks picking it for her bakery's walls. They'd made *her* lilac their wedding color. Or it was a big coincidence, and she was gnawing on the bamboo cocktail pick for nothing.

She needed another drink. Before she could reach the bar, a man who wore glasses and looked sort of like the direct-to-video version of Michael Ealy approached and said, "Hey, I'm Gordon. I'm filming guests' messages to the happy couple."

Retta looked at the man and the smartphone he wielded. "What sort of message?"

"Well wishes mostly. But if you have embarrassing stories, that'll do too," Gordon said, chuckling at his own suggestion. "The video will be played during the reception on the wedding day."

Retta was on edge, but a clip like that would definitely help emphasize to everyone she'd moved on. "Sure."

"Great. Let's do it on the balcony and get some of that natural light."

She hobbled outside and stood there with her empty cocktail glass waiting for further instructions.

"All right," he said, holding up the phone's camera to her face. "Action."

Retta looked at the tiny lens and wished she still had a drink to throw back. "Hey, congratulations. Wishing you two nothing but the best."

Gordon nodded and gave a thumbs up. "Okay, good. Could you give me a bit more?"

"More?" Retta asked.

"Yeah, you know… More."

Retta nodded and reset her smile. "Hey, Irene and

Christopher! I'm so excited for you to take this huge step. All the best in the future."

"Better," Gordon said, looking down at the footage he'd captured. "Other people have been throwing in a quick story about the couple as well."

Did this man not understand she was playing a delicate game? She took a moment to find a story and proceeded to ramble on for two minutes about a silly childhood memory of Irene.

"Again, congratulations," Retta said at the end of the spiel, raising her empty glass.

"Do you have anything to say to the groom?" the man asked.

This was starting to feel like an interrogation. Who'd sent this Gordon dude, anyway?

Retta nonchalantly shook her head.

"What about—"

"Hey, man. I think you got enough footage from her."

Both Gordon and Retta jumped as they looked over to find Duncan standing there watching them. A knot in her stomach untangled seeing him.

"You're right. You're right," Gordon said, bowing over clasped hands. "Thanks for your time."

Duncan drew nearer. He'd gotten a shape up and the dark suit he wore fit him perfectly.

"Hi," he said as he leaned in to hug her. "Sorry, I'm late."

It was for show, obviously, but she couldn't deny the goosebumps that appeared across her arms as his hand made contact with her bare back and he planted a kiss on her cheek.

"It's fine," she said, hoping she didn't sound breathless.

"I was trying to find parking, believe it or not," he said, before looking her up and down. "You look beautiful."

Again, with the goosebumps. "Anything looks good when it's not covered in flour," she said, laughing through the sudden nerves.

He smiled from one side of his mouth.

"Actually," Retta said, digging for her phone in her small purse. "Could you take a photo of me real quick? I need to send it to my friend who's the reason I even bought this."

Nia wanted to see the full ensemble, and Retta knew she'd not look as put together by the end of the evening when she in all likelihood spilled something on herself. Duncan took her phone and stood a distance away from her as she leaned up against the railing.

He didn't give her a countdown or anything, so she awkwardly stood there, smiling. However, her smile dropped when her cousin, Monica, from out of nowhere, stepped in front of her and said, "Oh my God. You came."

Chapter Thirteen

"WHY DIDN'T you tell me you were coming?" Monica asked, swatting her arm. "We could've carpooled."

"Yeah, sorry. I've been a little busy," Retta said, sending Duncan a glance.

"Does that mean you're coming to the wedding too?" her younger cousin asked, taking a sip of her drink.

"Yup, I'll be there."

"Very mature of you," she whispered.

Monica's sister, Natalie, appeared as suddenly with a martini glass in hand and humongous sunglasses on top of her 'fro. "Hey, I didn't expect to see you here."

"I wouldn't miss it," Retta replied, wondering how many variations of that sentence she'd have to say this evening.

"Of course not," Monica said, surveying the dress Retta wore. "This is different for you. Is it new?"

Retta looked down at the formfitting black dress, ignoring the price tag digging into her armpit. "Relatively."

"Cute," Monica replied, brushing the fabric with the back of her hand.

"All right, enough chit chat. Let's get down to business," Natalie said, pulling out her phone. "I found out two of the five groomsmen are single. Also, the best man has a brother who, based on my intel, won't be here tonight but will be at the wedding."

There was a group chat that Retta had unceremoniously been added to after getting dumped by Chris. She'd quickly discovered it was a place her cousins and a bunch of their single friends ranted about the dating scene. They also periodically acted as each other's wingwoman at events and parties.

"So we don't step on each other's toes, who are you most drawn to?" Natalie asked.

"I'm good," Retta said, sending Duncan another glance. He stood patiently a few paces away, watching them. She hoped he wasn't catching any of this conversation.

The two sisters looked at each other then back to Retta.

"That's okay," Monica said, rubbing Retta's bare arm. "Maybe next time."

"Yeah, we didn't mean to rush you. We thought since you showed up, you were over Ch—"

Retta coughed. "It's not that. I'd actually like you to meet someone."

Her cousins turned in the direction she pointed.

Duncan walked up and showcased his dimpled smile before saying, "Duncan Gilmore. Retta's boyfriend."

She held her breath waiting for her cousins to object, laugh, or call her a liar. But both of their eyes widened as they looked between her and her supposed man. There was a general greeting made, but Retta could sense they were formulating no less than fifteen questions.

"Is that any good?" Duncan asked, looking at Natalie's drink.

Her cousin nodded with her mouth agape, presenting her glass as if offering him a sip.

"Cool, I think I'll go get one," he said, smiling again. "It was nice meeting you both."

For a moment Retta thought he was going to leave her there, but he took her hand in his and moved them toward the bar inside the condo. More guests had arrived while she'd been on the balcony, and every corner of the interior was lively. She avoided eye contact by taking a keen interest in the wooden floors.

"You okay?" Duncan asked as they joined the line in front of the bar.

"Yeah. Why?"

"You've not looked up once, your hand is clammy, and your grip is cutting off circulation."

She removed her hand from his and wiped it down the front of her dress. "I'm fine."

But after they'd gotten their drinks, she could admit she was a little skittish. The reality of what they were trying to pull off was hitting her. Plus, she was noticing more lilac decorations.

They moved to an unoccupied corner of the home, and she peered over her glass, trying to see if she caught anyone staring.

"I feel like people can tell we're frauds," she whispered.

"No one can tell," Duncan said before moving his body to block her view of the party. "Look at me." His voice dropped, and she was compelled to meet his gaze. "Nobody can tell. Breathe."

She nodded.

"No, I mean breathe right now. Inhale for three-seconds then exhale," he said.

He encouraged her to keep going. However, the deep breathing in addition to their proximity made her feel like she was being hypnotized. They were standing so close she could see the nick on his chin he most likely got from shaving.

"Hey, if making out would help you relax, I'm down," he said as she realized it looked like she'd been studying his mouth.

She rolled her eyes despite not hating the idea at all. By the end of the short practice, she felt better but slightly embarrassed that he had to calm her down in the first place. She's the one who brought him here. This was her scheme.

"Thanks," she said.

A screechy voice, amplified by a microphone, cut through the noise of the party and drew their attention.

"Hello!" Chris's mom, Mrs. Washington, said from under the balloon archway near the dance floor.

The woman had a sunny disposition and an affinity for broaches. The last time Retta had seen her ex's mother was Christmas two years ago. She'd always gotten the sense the older woman didn't totally like her. It was all the vaguely insulting comments she used to make about Retta's clothes.

"Welcome, everybody," Mrs. Washington said as the room quieted down. "Dinner will start as soon as the bride and groom arrive, so please grab a seat... And maybe pace yourself, Anita."

A woman, presumably Anita, gave a thumbs-up as she continued to chug the contents of her wine glass.

"Where do you want to sit?" Duncan asked.

She looked at the two long tables and pointed at seats closest to the bar. As they neared, however, it became clear the spots were reserved.

"Let's try over there," Duncan said as they walked toward the middle.

At this point, all she wanted to do was relieve her aching feet.

"Are these taken?" Retta asked a woman with light brown skin in her sixties who sat nearby. She wore a mesh shawl and silver earrings too heavy for her earlobes.

"No, all yours," the woman said.

As Retta settled into the chair, she relaxed a bit. She disappeared sitting at the expansive table. Duncan's arm was casually draped over the back of her seat, and the cologne he wore, a scent she could only describe as fresh, wafted toward her every time he shifted.

"I've never been to anything like this," Duncan said, picking up the monogrammed napkin from the plate in front of him. "This isn't even the wedding."

"The groom's parents are pretty showy."

Duncan huffed.

"You look familiar," the woman with the heavy earrings said to Retta.

She didn't recognize her at all, but she supposed it was possible. "I'm Irene's cousin, Retta."

"Oh, yes. I can see the resemblance." The older woman offered her hand. "It's around the eyes. I'm Margaret, Christopher's godmother."

Retta smiled while Duncan introduced himself. She was glad she'd lucked out and was seated next to someone who didn't seem aware of her history with Chris.

"I was skeptical about them pulling off this wedding in two months, but—" Margaret looked around the condo—

"It looks incredible. Sometimes you're so in love waiting doesn't make sense."

Retta was about to reply with one of her canned responses when Duncan said, "But it's probably best not to rush into things, right? Who's to say you wouldn't later discover you're incompatible?"

The older woman shrugged. "Well, that's what divorce is for."

Duncan opened his mouth like he might say something else, but he simply smiled.

"Are you a part of the wedding party, love?" Margaret asked.

"Me? God, no," Retta said too quickly, before clearing her throat. "I mean, it's not my thing."

Margaret nodded, seriously. "Oh, I understand. The first half of the 80s, all my girlfriends got married. It takes a certain personality to handle that much tulle… I'm afraid I didn't handle it very well."

Before Retta could ask any follow-up questions, loud applause swept the room.

"Speaking of lovebirds," the older woman said, pointing toward the entrance of the condo.

Irene and Chris stood in the spacious entryway in matching white outfits, smiling and greeting their guests. Barbie and Ken wished they were so polished. When Retta had been with Chris, she'd often joke about being the dust bunny on his coattails.

She turned away from the scene, trying to look like she'd received the most riveting text message. Opening up to her photos, she studied the ones Duncan had taken of her on the balcony. One was a full body shot and the other one was a close up of her face.

"I think I might have a second career in photography," Duncan said, peering down at her phone.

She smiled, zooming into the amateur pictures to reveal how unfocused the images actually were.

"Picky, picky," he said, and another wave of calmness flowed through her.

Duncan was here. She wasn't doing this evening alone. But even if she was, how many times had she been in the same room as her ex and her cousin? She was here to be seen and prove a point. That didn't include having an involved conversation with either of them.

"Oh, don't you two look beautiful," Margaret said.

Retta looked up to find Irene and Chris pulling out the seats across from her and Duncan.

Of course.

———

The pressure of their ruse was obviously getting to Retta. Her posture was stiff, her smile too wide, and she'd taken to bouncing her knee. But Duncan hoped these details were only noticeable to him because he sat so close.

Introductions were made, and his first impression of Retta's cousin was that she seemed sweet. She was the type who giggled at the end of every other sentence. Her fiancé, on the other hand, had an arrogant tilt to his chin and off-putting way of swirling the ice in his glass.

"How's wedding planning going?" Margaret asked.

"Good, I think," Irene said as she laughed and gently racked her hand through her straightened hair. "But I won't lie. I've thought of calling off the whole thing and going to the courthouse."

"You wanted big. We're going big," Christopher said as they turned to each other and rubbed their noses together.

"Good man. Spoil her early and often," Margaret said.

But the pair were so engaged with their public display of affection, they didn't hear a thing. It got uncomfortable.

"Are we doing this couple thing wrong?" Duncan whispered, leaning in as if he was about to press his nose to Retta's.

"Don't you dare," she said, her tense smile still in place.

"How's the bakery doing?" Irene asked after she physically separated from her husband-to-be.

Margaret turned to Retta. "You own a bakery?"

"I do."

"She's amazing," Duncan said, leaning forward to look at the older woman.

Irene nodded enthusiastically. "Babe, you really like those"—she waved her hand around her head as if to conjure up the word—"I can't remember what they're called."

"Financiers," Retta and Christopher said at the same time.

Her bouncing knee stilled, and there was a sustained silence as she and the groom looked at each other. Duncan squinted. What was going on?

They moved on from the strange moment when someone with a high pitched voice let everyone know dinner was served.

While standing in line, they were approached several times. You'd think Retta had appeared through wizardry the way people reacted to her presence.

"Holy shit. You came," a woman with a pixie cut and large hoop earrings said as she passed them on her way to the back of the queue.

While they were picking their dinner rolls, an older man interrupted and said, "I thought my eyes were playing tricks on me when I spotted you earlier."

After the third interaction like that, Duncan made a mental note to ask Retta about it later.

Back at their table, they found the bride and groom's parents sitting next to their respective child.

"This might be the nicest thing I've ever seen you wear, Retta," Mrs. Washington said as she settled a napkin across her lap.

Retta responded with a stilted laugh.

Irene's mother, Wendy, gestured between the two of them. "How long has this been going on?"

They'd never discussed the nitty-gritty details of their "relationship", and Duncan would've let Retta take the lead if she'd actually said anything.

"A few months, right, baby?" Duncan said.

She looked up long enough to smile and nod.

"Months?" the mother-of-the-bride asked. "You sneaky girl. When I was at the bakery the last time, you were acting so coy. I even told Clifton"—she patted the man next to her—"I didn't think you had a plus one."

"We were trying to take things slow," Duncan said after Retta only managed to stutter. He placed his hand over her knee, stilling its movement. "We work next door to each other and didn't want to make things weird if it didn't work out."

"Oh?" Irene asked, stopping with her fork halfway to her mouth. "You work at the spa?"

"Those were the previous owners. I own a boxing gym with my business partner."

"Explains the muscles," Margaret said with a wink.

The conversation briefly diverged from what Duncan did for work but returned when someone several seats down asked the engaged couple where they were going on their honeymoon.

"New Zealand," Irene replied, clapping her hands and practically bouncing in her seat.

"New Zealand?" Retta squeaked.

She said it so loudly and like it was a cuss word that everyone involved in the conversation turned to look at her.

Shrinking in her seat, Retta said, "I've always wanted to go."

"Well. Um," the bride said, fidgeting with her cutlery. "I'm sure you'll go one day."

"Duncan," Irene's mother said. "Your gym would be perfect for building stamina, right?"

"Mom."

The older woman waved off her daughter's protest and said, "They're doing a lot of hiking on their honeymoon, and Irene mentioned that she wanted to build up her stamina."

"Definitely," Duncan said, placing his fork and knife down. "A lot of our classes are suitable for all fitness levels as well."

"Do you have a business card?" Irene's mother asked.

Grabbing one from his wallet, he presented it to the bride. "No pressure."

Irene glanced at Retta before accepting it. "Thanks."

"I've never understood boxing or any other sport where grown men hit each other," Christopher said, taking a slow drink from his glass. "Seems mindless."

Before Duncan could defend his sport, Retta said, "It's not just about force or power. It also requires a lot of skill and agility."

Something warm bloomed inside Duncan in response to her words.

The groom shrugged, and it felt more dismissive than if he'd said something outright insulting. But what did he care about the opinion of a random man?

"You must enjoy having each other so close by," Margaret said, nudging Retta with her shoulder.

"She definitely takes advantage of it more than I do," Duncan said, laughing. "Recently, she came over unannounced for one of my full body conditioning classes."

Retta jumped in her seat as if she'd been pinched.

He turned to her with a very serious expression and asked, "Is everything okay?"

"Screw you," she mumbled, hiding a smile behind her napkin.

"Sorry, I didn't quite catch that," he said, leaning in.

This was the first time all night he'd seen Retta truly at ease. He was happy he could at least provide her a bit of respite.

As the catering staff cleared their plates, Retta pointed to his elbow and said, "You got sauce on your jacket."

Duncan twisted his arm to take a look. This was his one and only suit, and he planned to wear it to the wedding as well. "I'll be right back."

Getting up, he headed toward the back of the condo where he'd spotted a washroom.

He found a small line up in front of the door. While he waited, he smiled to himself about the night so far. They were really pulling this thing off.

His ears perked up when the two people directly behind him mentioned Retta. He turned his head and found a middle-aged man and woman studying him.

"Sorry," the woman with long red acrylic nails said. She leaned forward and whispered, "You're Retta's new man, right?"

"Yeah," Duncan said, the word sliding from his mouth with very little effort.

"I was just telling him how it's real big of you to show up," the woman said.

The man crossed his arms and sucked his teeth. "It couldn't be me though. An ex stays in the past. You don't go to their weddings."

Duncan paused for many seconds as his brain worked to draw a conclusion. It came as the restroom door opened.

Chapter Fourteen

UPON REENTERING the hub of the party with a clean jacket, a burning sensation stirred in Duncan's chest. Everything made sense now. The awkward introductions, the tense exchanges, Retta's anxiety. There had to be unresolved feelings there. Why else would she be here and require his presence?

People had abandoned their seats to grab dessert and mingle, but Retta was still seated at the table with Margaret.

"Sorry to interrupt," he said as the two women looked up. "I'm going to steal her for a moment."

Margaret sat back and winked at Retta. "Go ahead, love."

Standing up, she squeezed the older woman's arm before turning to Duncan and saying, "We can't leave now."

"We're not," he said as he guided her to the dim semi-populated dance floor.

They found a spot amongst the people swaying to

smooth jazz. He hooked his arms around her waist, and she placed her hands on his shoulders.

Retta's feelings were none of his business. The new information was irrelevant, and he wouldn't bring it up. He had one job to do tonight: be the best fake boyfriend.

"This feels very '09 prom," she said after a few minutes.

"Ah-oh."

"No," she said, moving her head to look into his eyes. "I liked my prom."

They continued to sway until she faltered in her step. He held her fast.

"Sorry, it's these ridiculous shoes," she said, fixing her skewed glasses.

But she also seemed distracted by something over his shoulder. Duncan casually turned his head in that direction and found Christopher and Irene dancing on the other side of the room. The churning heat in his chest returned.

When he turned back, she was studying him, and for a moment he thought she'd figured out what he'd been told.

"You're playing the boyfriend role like a real thespian," she said, brushing his shoulders. "With your suit and everything."

"I had to borrow this tie."

She smiled. "I'm returning this dress."

He assessed the silky fabric that cascaded down her curves. "That's a shame. I like it."

Several seconds passed before she asked, "What do you like about it?"

Her warm breath snuck past his collar, sending shivers down his body. From the way her voice dropped, there was no mistaking the flirtation behind the question. Today had been rough for her; he understood that now. If she needed a distraction, he was willing to be that.

She incorrectly read his long pause because she shook her head and straightened. "Sorry, that's a weird question."

"No, it isn't," he said as he pulled her close to his body and pressed his face near her ear. "I like how flimsy and tearable it looks."

Her chest slowly rose and fell before she whispered, "Do you want to get out of here?"

Moving his thumb up and down her exposed back, he smiled and said, "I thought you wanted to stay."

She looked him in the eye before brushing her lips against his. "Now I want to leave."

An electrical current run between them as they said their farewells. It was as if they'd combust if they didn't get out of there.

He thought they were almost in the clear when she stopped mere paces from the door. "Ah," she said, turning to him. "You're about to meet my parents."

He knew who they were the moment he spotted them. When it came to meeting parents of people he dated, it never happened. To him, this step was a big move in a relationship, an ushering into the in-group. It came with pressure to please and impress people beyond his partner.

Duncan smiled and extended his hand out to Retta's parents. "Hi, Mr. and Mrs. Majors," he said to the two people before him. "It's nice to meet you."

They seemed pleasant, and he could see Retta in both of them. She got her mom's rounded nose and her father's large, expressive eyes. And both her parents were tall.

"Well, we're heading out," Retta said.

"But the party's just started," Mrs. Majors said.

"I know, but we both have early mornings," Retta said. "I'll call you later this weekend."

She hugged her parents, and he only had a literal

second to say goodbye himself. Duncan didn't know what the night would bring, but he knew once they left this place, nothing would be the same.

———

They calmly walked down the hallway, washed in yellow-tinged light. With each step they took toward the elevator, the butterflies in her stomach multiplied.

His hand on her open back was reassuring but maddening. She wanted more. He said this would happen when they'd been on his desk, but a part of her had thought it was something said in the heat of a moment. As soon as they entered the empty elevator and the doors closed behind them, Retta pushed Duncan against the wall.

She grabbed his head and brought his lips to hers as he pulled her leg up and around his waist. For several seconds, they shared fevered, heedless kisses before Duncan flipped her so she was the one pressed up against the elevator wall. His cologne, body, and touch all enveloped her.

The ping of the door opening on a different floor had them quickly separating. They demurely stood next to each other with the tips of their fingers the only thing in contact.

While a few people loaded onto the elevator, Duncan whispered, "Did you drive here?"

She nodded. "But we can take yours."

It was a long fifteen seconds to the parking level.

They were in his truck within minutes. But as much as she wanted to recline their chairs and go at it right then and there, two tall people were not comfortably fucking in that tight space.

"Your place or mine?" he asked, shoving the keys in the ignition.

"Whichever is closer."

He straightened in his seat and pulled out of the underground parking onto the road. The sound of people enjoying the downtown nightlife filled the otherwise quiet vehicle.

Duncan's hand came to rest on her exposed thigh. Her breathing slowed down as she watched his hand knead her flesh. When he began a laborious ascent up her thigh, she spread her legs as wide as the truck would allow.

Retta thought her heart might fly from her chest when he finally reached the outside of her damp panties. She closed her eyes and took a shuddering breath in the silence.

"How long have you been like this?" he asked, his voice sounding rough.

"Since we started dancing."

Duncan seemed spurred on by her answer. Even at the awkward angle, he was able to caress her into a state. There was something reckless about this, and she loved it. But she also wanted to make it to his apartment in one piece.

"Focus on the road," she said, pushing his hand away before pressing hers down the front of her underwear.

"Are you touching yourself?" Duncan asked.

"Yeah," she whispered, watching him as she circled her clit.

He looked away from the road to confirm her answer. "Fuck."

A low, breathy moan slipped past her lips.

"You're killing me here, Retta," he said.

"Sorry about that."

When she'd asked him to be her fake boyfriend, she'd expected him to do the bare minimum of performances.

But all night Duncan had been attentive, comforting, and entertaining. He'd gone above and beyond what was necessary.

With heavy lids, she watched his jaw clench and unclench. He held the steering wheel like he was trying to impress his hands into it. By the time they arrived at his apartment, she was on the verge of an orgasm. But he swiftly unfastened her seat belt and hauled her into his lap.

"This is what you want?" he asked, grabbing her hand to press to the front of his pants. "Me hard and risking speeding tickets for you?" His voice was distorted into a low bass that skated across her skin.

She brought her mouth to his, breathless from the knowledge he wanted her as much as she did him. They maneuvered themselves out of the vehicle without breaking or spraining anything, and they sped up the stairs to his apartment. It wasn't clear if Duncan locked the door behind them, but she was already circling her arms around his neck and kicking off her heels.

He groped for the light switch while guiding her into a bedroom where crisp air circulated.

"Last test?" she asked him, pushing the jacket off his shoulders.

Scattering kissing down her neck, he replied, "Three months ago. You?"

"January," she said, but her voice caught as he grabbed her ass and pulled her even closer to his hard body.

With clumsy fingers, Retta unbuttoned his shirt but quickly abandoned the tedious task to work on his pants. Her movements were rushed and fevered, but she slowed down once his trousers were off. His thighs, a testimony of the work he did every day, stood as unyielding columns. She dragged her fingers along them, feeling his coarse hair and hard flesh. And this was all before she got to his erection pressing against his briefs.

"You've gotta do something, baby. I'm trying to—"

He hissed as she finally pushed down his underwear. Her stomach actually fluttered seeing him in all his glory. Taking a hold of his dick from the base, she looked up as she placed her lips on the tip. His eyebrows drew closer together, his mouth fell open, and the veins in his neck made an appearance.

She used her tongue to tease the head before moving down the length. It was only when she returned to the top that she took him fully into her mouth.

His hand automatically traveled to the back of her head. He gently wrapped his fingers around her hair and guided her mouth over his dick at a steady pace. The sight of him with his head tilted back on the doors of his closet, sweat on his dark chest, and a smattering of hair that started at his navel was almost too much.

The low groans he made were loud and unencumbered. She felt them in her body, and they were enough for her to spread her legs and work her wetness around her clit.

Their gazes finally met, and she fucking loved him watching her suck.

"That pretty mouth, wants to take me all, huh?" he rasped.

It was the smile and the gentle way he cradled her head. It was tender. Too tender. It felt like that moment he was helping her calm down at the party. She didn't want this to be soul revealing or anything. It was just sex.

Relaxing her jaw and flattening her tongue, she pressed herself forward even farther, feeling every vein and contour fill the space in her mouth. Duncan's smile dropped, and the grip on her hair tightened as he quickened the pace.

"Dammit, Retta," he shouted after she increased the suction and dug her fingers into the side of his thighs.

Without warning, he pulled his dick from her mouth, dragged her upwards by her shoulders, and kissed her deeply. He guided her to his bed, and the sound of her dress ripping filled the room as she fell backward onto the mattress.

"Did you get that pussy ready for me?" he asked, hovering over her with strong arms on either side of her head. "I want to slide right in."

His words settled on her like molten lava. She could only manage to nod as he removed her soaked panties and tossed them over his shoulder.

While he worked to remove her dress, his gaze fixed onto her chest for several seconds. For a moment, Retta thought he'd become overwhelmed by the absolute beauty of her modest chest. But when she took a look at them herself, she saw the flesh-colored nipple coverings she'd worn with the backless outfit.

"Oh, just," she slowly peeled each pastie off and flung them somewhere to the left of her, "done."

"There they are," he said, briefly rubbing his thumbs over them.

When he dropped to his knees in front of her open legs, she thought he'd go straight to her pussy, but he started on the inside of her left knee and worked his way up with soft love bites and kisses. Each one sent her deeper into the embrace of her desire. Her capacity to breathe waned as he neared where she wanted him to be.

His warm breath caressed her and elicited a shiver that made her toes curl and her back arch.

"Look at you," he rasped, moving his fingers along her slit before holding them up for her to bear witness to her own need.

The sound of him breathing her in was almost her undoing. "Please, Duncan."

Lowering his head, he gave her a long lick that ended at her clit.

"Oh, God," she said, her head flopping backward.

She felt him smile as he closed his mouth around her sensitive bud and swirled his tongue. As she edged closer to her release, she fisted the sheets and tried to prolong the moment. But seconds later, everything tightened and she was catapulted into an orgasm.

While she recovered, he reached into the drawer of his side table to retrieve a condom. She watched him as he deftly rolled the latex on. He positioned himself over her, bracketing her torso with his arms. As he placed his dick at her slick entrance their eyes locked. She told herself to look away, but the focus and interest he was studying her face with made it impossible.

Her eyelids lowered as he slid ever so slowly into her. She clamped her lips together to avoid moaning his name. He withdrew his dick from her pussy only to drive into her once again just as slow but with more force. She whimpered as she felt him stretch and fill her. Pleasure permeated her body.

Every time he retreated and entered her something in her lower belly tightened. Her clit had a pulse of its own, and her skin grew damp and heated.

Digging her short fingernails into his lower back she whispered, "Faster."

He gave her that crooked smile of his before he straightened and hooked one of her legs over his arm. This sent him sliding deeper inside of her.

"Yeah, like that," she said as she grabbed her own breasts.

He barely gave her a chance to adjust to the new position before he started fucking her at an unrelenting speed.

"This good?" he asked, watching her with a fierce expression.

She didn't answer right away, occupied with the jolts of pleasure.

"Huh?" he asked again as he leaned forward until their foreheads touched.

"So good. Don't you dare stop."

His continued caresses and movement inside her triggered sounds and moans that came from the depth of her body.

"That's right, baby," he said without ceasing his powerful thrusts. "Get loud."

She could see the light. It was beckoning her to surrender. She needed a few more—

"I got you," Duncan whispered, reaching between their bodies for her clit and kissing her chin. "Let go."

And like her body had been waiting for his permission, an orgasm ripped through her that couldn't help but be expressed in a scream. Her body seized, and she held onto Duncan's firm torso as she let ecstasy run its course.

He was still fucking her when he scooped her up closer to his chest. She kissed his shoulder and held on tight until he came on loud grunts and a shout.

And for a long time, all that was heard was their heavy breathing.

————

There'd been a brief moment after Retta had fallen asleep where Duncan's instinct to flee had surfaced. Don't get him wrong, fucking Retta had been amazing. So much so, they'd done it two more times before finally settling down to sleep.

But this quiet moment where he held her long after their bodies had recovered from orgasms wasn't what he was used to. It was too intimate, something reserved for people who made five-year plans with their partners. However, as he now lost feeling in his arm from being the big spoon, he could admit he didn't want to spend the early hours of Sunday any other way.

What helped with this unusual calm and acceptance of such intimacy was the knowledge that this wasn't a real relationship and Retta was still hung up on her ex-boyfriend. There'd be no attachments on either side at the end of this. Or at least that's what he told himself as he drifted off to sleep, breathing in the lingering perfume on her skin.

———

In the morning, Duncan woke up to Retta's warm body pressing up against his and her long limbs entangled in the sheets. He ran kisses down her exposed arm, loving the way she leaned into his touch, even in sleep. Dragging himself out of bed, he took a shower and got ready for the day. When he returned to his room, he found her sitting on the edge of the bed scrolling through her phone with the sheet around her torso and her hair in disarray.

"You don't mind if I borrow some clothes, do you?" she asked, nodding to her rumpled dress in the corner.

He grinned. "Pick whatever you want."

"How magnanimous," she said as she stood up, pulling the bedding with her.

God, it had only been a few hours, but seeing Retta

draped in white fabric like some Grecian goddess had him wanting to drag her back to bed.

"If you like that," he said, advancing toward her. "You'll be pleased to know I'm making breakfast, *and* there's an unused toothbrush in the left drawer in the bathroom."

She took a step forward and kissed him on the cheek. "Thanks."

Forget what they'd done all night, that gesture left him feeling light and peppy. Once she disappeared into the bathroom, he moved to the kitchen to start a simple breakfast.

"I think you win the Who Wore It Better contest," Retta said after she reemerged thirty minutes later, showered and in his t-shirt and shorts.

"Not even close."

They probably would've stood there staring at each other for a while if the toast hadn't sprung from the toaster, pulling them out their weird trance.

Retta relieved him of a plate of scrambled eggs and found a spot on the high stools at his counter. "What would you be doing today if—"

"If I wasn't catering to you?" he asked, bringing along the toast and condiments.

"Please," she said, reaching for the hot sauce.

Chuckling, he said, "I probably would've gone for a run, taken a shower, then headed to the gym to do some work."

She nodded. "Sounds like what I expected."

"I see you waking up early as you usually do and painting," Duncan said, taking a large bite from the toast he'd smashed avocado on.

She stilled. "How do you know that?"

He shrugged. "You told me that you wanted to pursue

painting when you were younger. I assume you still enjoy it."

"I do," she said, smiling.

They ate in silence for a little before she said, "Oh, did you get my email about the wedding weekend?"

"I saw it," he said. "We're staying at your grandmother's place, right?"

"Yes, and I can't stress enough how important it is for you to call her Ms. Edie or ma'am. She hates when people who aren't her actual grandchildren call her Granny or Grandma."

"Don't worry, older women love me."

Retta shook her head so hard that he thought her glasses would fall off her face. "My grandmother isn't the press-you-to-her-bosom type of lady. She's sometimes cranky, doesn't know a cookie recipe, and she'll tell you what she feels without provocation."

She sounded like Anthony.

"Got it," he said.

After they'd finished and cleared their breakfast, Duncan got his wallet and keys. "I need to drop something off at my dad's place. It's on the way. It'll take seconds."

"That's okay," Retta said.

The drive was quick, and when they arrived at the quaint townhouse his father now lived in, Duncan retrieved the box of power tools from the back of his truck. His dad had been bugging him to return them since he was starting projects around his home. Jogging up the stairs to the front porch, Duncan took note of the fresh paint on the door trim before knocking.

His father almost immediately answered as if he'd been expecting him, but asked, "Hey, what're you doing here?"

"Dropping these off," he replied, raising the box.

Only after narrowing how open the door was, did his

father reach for his belongings. "Thanks. You have a good day now, son."

"You, too," he said, slowly.

As he was about to turn and head back to his vehicle, someone from inside the house said, "Malcolm, don't forget to tip."

Duncan froze, recognizing the voice immediately. His mother opened the door, emerging from inside the townhouse swathed in a large fuzzy robe.

His dad's head dropped, and his mom's eyes widened as she started talking quickly.

"Unbelievable."

"Duncan, honey—"

"I swear to God if you two are getting back together…"

They didn't say anything, and Duncan laughed humorlessly before turning around and striding back to his car.

Retta seemed to sense something was up because she didn't say a word. He barely took the time to fasten his seatbelt before driving off.

All he could do was focus on the road and the feeling of the steering wheel under his hands.

"You took the wrong turn," Retta said after several minutes.

He shook his head. "Sorry."

Quickly, he found his way back onto the correct road, and as they neared the intersection across from the condo, Retta said, "None of my business, but I'm compelled as your fake girlfriend to ask if you're okay."

He was about to brush off her inquiry, but as he pulled up behind her parked car on the side of the road, she didn't look like she was asking out of obligation. Her eyebrows were drawn together, and her body was almost fully turned toward him.

"My parents are the last people who should reconcile," he said. "They've given marriage a shot and proved time and time again it doesn't work between them."

"I'm sorry," she said.

"Nah, it's fine. I think I'm just pissed about how they have my sister and me writing speeches for their divorce party. It's—"

"Oh, crap, I'm about to get a ticket," Retta said, removing her seatbelt and pointing to the parking enforcement officer advancing toward her car.

She looked at him. "Call me and we can finish this conversation, okay?"

But even as she made the sincere offer, he knew they both knew he wouldn't be doing that. And maybe that's why she leaned over and kissed him before exiting his truck.

Chapter Fifteen

AFTER SPENDING several hours in a birthing class, Kym and Retta found a spot outside of a chic Italian cafe where they could eat their gelato. The sound of street performers and bicycle bells accompanied the breeze Retta was happy to feel on this warm day.

"Thanks for coming with me," Kym said.

Len had been unable to make the class because of work, and Retta had stepped in to take notes and be there for her friend. However, she hadn't anticipated the amount of information that would be thrown at her and how over-whelming it all was.

Several times throughout the class, she had to conceal her panicked responses. She wasn't the one about to give birth, after all.

"No, problem," Retta said. "It was…"

"A lot?" Kym asked, smiling.

"Yeah. Jesus. So much."

Her friend laughed, spooning some gelato into her mouth. "How was the engagement party?"

Oh, yes. The engagement party.

"It was great," Retta said. There was no controlling the inflection on the last word.

"Good. That's good," Kym said. "Your family bought it?"

"Yeah, I think so."

"So, it's all going according to plan?"

Retta stabbed her frozen dessert with the spoon and took a breath. "Nope, I like him. Like really like him."

Kym removed her sunglasses and looked at her. "Shit."

"Yup."

She realized it after she'd arrived home from spending the night with him. While folding laundry and cleaning her apartment, she caught herself smiling and unable to focus on the podcast playing.

"If you're feeling it, he's probably too. Maybe you guys can actually start dating."

Retta shook her head. "He doesn't want that."

"He told you?"

Looking out into the distance, Retta said, "Yeah, he likes short and casual relationships."

And it was understandable, given the drama he witnessed between his parents.

"But people change their minds. Circumstances change them," Kym said, scraping the bottom of her cup. "Look at me. I've purchased tutus for the baby. Do you hear me? I bought my baby tutus in four different colors, Ret. Pre-pregnancy Kymberlé wouldn't dream of purchasing something so impractical."

"Yeah, but that's a personal shift. I can't expect that from him."

Her friend studied her for a moment. "So, that's it? You're going to end it after the wedding without even having a conversation?"

Shrugging, Retta said, "Yeah, I'm not opening up

simply to get rejected." She could imagine Duncan being so sweet about it too. "It's not like I'm in love with him. I'll enjoy the sex—"

"The sex?" Kym practically shouted.

A few people sitting around them turned, including a dog at his owner's feet.

Retta awkwardly smiled at the strangers. "I don't think you said that loud enough."

"Sorry," Kym responded, lowering her voice. "I thought you two were doing this Hallmark Movie style. You know, chaste kiss here. Hand on waist there."

"Yeah, it started that way."

Now they were doing other things the FCC wouldn't care for.

"But I'm going after emotionally available men when this is through," Retta said.

"Fair."

"Like Steve. He's—"

"Steve? When did Steve come back into the picture?"

"Oh, did I forget to tell you he didn't actually ghost me?"

"Ah, yeah," Kym replied, frowning as she leaned forward.

"I didn't enter his number correctly in my phone," Retta said.

"And?"

"And he asked me out again when I bumped into him, and I might take him up on his offer later."

"But if you're open to something with Steve, and he's interested in you, why not take him to the wedding instead?" Kym asked.

"B-because I've already committed to Duncan."

Kym wiped her hands on the napkin. "Yeah, that's what I'm worried about."

———

As Duncan pulled up to his mother's house, a different sort of anxiety settled over him than usual. They were supposed to move his father's belongings to his new home, but after what he saw days before, he wondered if this wasn't actually a gathering where his parents would announce they'd decided to remain married.

Entering the house, he could hear his sister and father downstairs. A good sign. They were probably working through his father's extensive library.

Moving through the kitchen to get to the basement, he found his mother still in her bonnet sitting at the kitchen island with an open book in front of her.

His dad happened to emerge from the basement at that moment carrying a basin full of papers. All three of them looked at one another for a moment before simultaneously opening their mouths to speak. But nothing came out.

"What's going on?" Gwen said, following behind their dad up the stairs with a garbage bag slung over her shoulder. "Why is everyone being weird?"

"I was about to ask them whether or not the divorce is still happening," Duncan said.

Gwen's eyes widened as she looked between them. "Wait, what? Why wouldn't—"

"I found Mom at Dad's place."

The bag his sister held dropped to the tiled floor with a soft thud. "Are you serious?"

His mother closed her book and got up from her seat. "Yes, of course the divorce is still happening."

"Yeah?" Duncan asked skeptically, folding his arms.

"No, for real. I don't want to be here in three weeks bringing back your stuff, Dad," Gwen said.

His father released a robust laugh. "The divorce papers are drawn. Things are being settled. Trust us."

Their mother nodded. "And I know you might interpret some things as signs that we won't go through with it, but you have to understand your dad and I have known each other for so long that it's sometimes easier to sleep with—"

"Nope," Gwen said.

"We can end it right there," Duncan said, squeezing past his father to get to the basement.

The conversation at least temporarily assuaged his fears of a divorce cancelation, and he settled in for the long chore of sorting and packing his father's belongings.

An hour in, Duncan held up a decorative silver tray and said, "Dad."

His father studied the item for a long time, and Duncan was about to put it in the "I don't know" pile when he said, "It's your Mom's."

"Look what I found," Gwen said from the other corner of the basement. She was seated cross-legged on the ground with a photo album in her lap.

Both he and his father approached and stood behind her.

Gwen laughed as she pointed to an increasingly degenerating photo of their father with a huge afro and an aggressively popped collar.

As his sister kept flipping the pages, Duncan enjoyed seeing pictures he'd never known existed.

There was one where his dad was definitely smoking a blunt and another one where he lay on the hood of a car. Some of the pictures featured their mother. In one she was eating ice cream and sporting a 'fro similar to his father's in the previous image.

"This is when we went to Niagara in seventy-nine," his

dad said, pointing at the picture of them in front of the waterfalls. "We'd recently started working at a school together."

Another photo showed them on a veranda somewhere drinking cola in glass bottles.

"You guys look so happy," Gwen said, running her fingers over the photos trapped under the thin plastic.

His father huffed, but it was true. They did look happy.

The next page held a photograph that had been carelessly sealed under the film. It was a family portrait they'd taken back when Duncan was a preteen.

"God, I remember this day," Gwen said.

He did too. They'd gone to the large Walmart on the other side of town to take them. The trip unfolded as usual with his parents arguing over something.

Duncan shook his head. "Felt bad for that photographer."

However, none of the drama of that day was evident in the glossy final product. It looked like a stock image you'd find on a brochure in a doctor's office.

Seeing these photos was a good reminder not to get fooled by the veneer of relationships. He needed that dose of cynicism especially since he'd been creating a fantasy with Retta that he found increasingly alluring.

The sound of descending footsteps pulled Duncan out of his thoughts, and the three of them turned toward the staircase.

"I didn't realize how much stuff we'd accumulated," his mother said, laughing lightly.

There wasn't a spot on the floor that wasn't covered with stuff.

"We'll have to pick this up next weekend," Gwen said.

"I actually won't be able to help out next weekend,"

Duncan said, avoiding eye contact by flipping through a decade-old magazine.

"Oh?" his mom asked.

"I'm out of town," he replied vaguely.

"For what?" his father asked as he added a desk lamp to the "keep" stack.

"A wedding."

Everyone turned to him.

"A wedding?" his mother asked. "Whose wedding?"

"A friend's cousin's wedding."

He'd let them draw their own conclusions.

"Is the friend that woman I met a few weeks ago? What's her name?" his sister said, pausing for a moment before snapping her fingers. "Retta."

Dammit.

"Yeah, it's her cousin's wedding."

"Retta?" his dad asked.

His mom walked further into the basement. "Is she a trainer at your gym?"

"No, she owns the bakery next door to Spotlight," Gwen said before he could.

Duncan sensed the forthcoming questions so he said, "And yes, she's strictly a friend."

(If a friend was someone you made come and pretended to date.)

His statement eliminated any interest his parents had in discussing Retta. A good thing too considering this was most likely the last time he'd ever bring her up.

Chapter Sixteen

THE TWO AND half hour drive to the small town of Cedar Lake was uneventful for Duncan. He passed the main part of town to enter a more rural area where Retta's grandmother lived. His GPS seemed unsure where it was leading him, and it didn't help that the sun had set and there were no street lights.

When Duncan pulled up to a modest house and saw no sign of Retta's small gray car, he texted her. As he'd told her, he was good with older women, and he had no problem going up to the door and introducing himself to her grandmother. However, he wasn't positive he was in the right place.

It must've been close to thirty minutes later when Retta finally appeared and parked right behind him. He hadn't realized he'd been worried until the muscles in his neck relaxed.

"Hey, sorry," Retta said, pulling a tiny suitcase from her car. "I had to get gas."

"All good," he said, refusing to acknowledge his desire to hug her.

As they walked to the dark house Retta said, "Remember, Ms. Edie or ma'am."

She pressed the doorbell, and a dog inside barked in response. When the front door opened, a woman in her seventies stood there in a matching navy tracksuit with jet black curls that hit her chin. A chocolate lab lumbered a few steps behind.

"I expected you an hour ago," the older woman said, frowning.

"Hi, Granny," Retta said, kissing the older woman's cheek before crouching low to pet and rub the dog. "Hi, Levi, baby."

Ms. Edie beckoned them inside with her hands. "Get in, get in, before the mosquitos swarm."

They both entered the house, and Retta said, "Granny, this is Duncan… My boyfriend."

"Boyfriend?" Retta's grandmother asked incredulously, giving him a good look up and down. "You told me a friend?"

"No, Granny. I said boyfriend."

"Well, you're not sleeping together under my roof," she said. "The walls are too thin for all that. Not that the two of you could fit in the twin bed anyway. What are you? Six four?" Ms. Edie asked Duncan.

"Six three, ma'am. And it's nice to meet you. I can see where Retta gets her beauty from."

The older woman snorted. "Did you warn him shit like that doesn't work on me?"

"I did," Retta said, rubbing her forehead.

Okay, so, Ms. Edie was tough.

"Drop your things there, and I'll show you around after we've eaten," the older woman said.

"How's the weather been?" Retta asked her grandmother.

"Really, Coretta, the weather?"

Retta laughed. "I'm genuinely interested."

"The Internet can give you everything you want to know about the weather here going back a century—"

Ms. Edie had stopped mid-sentence to stare at Duncan's sneaker-clad feet. At first, he thought she might be admiring them, but there wasn't an accompanying comment.

Retta made a polite cough and said under her breath, "Your shoes. Take off your shoes."

Duncan looked down. Retta had removed hers and Ms. Edie was wearing house slippers.

"Shi—" he said, catching himself before he swore. "My bad."

He removed his sneakers right there and walked them back to the front area. So the first impression was a bust.

They sat down at a small dining room table as Ms. Edie placed a cold looking dish of spaghetti in the center.

"Let me reheat this in the oven," Retta said as she headed to the kitchen with the ceramic.

Duncan smiled at Ms. Edie who responded with an assessing look.

"Where did you meet?" The older woman asked, sipping something from a mug.

"He and his business partner opened a boxing gym next door to the bakery," Retta said from the kitchen.

"Do you love her?" Ms. Edie asked.

Duncan almost choked on the frankly bitter lemonade she'd served. "I-I—"

"Granny, please stop harassing him," Retta said as she returned to her seat.

"It was just a question."

Thankfully, the conversation during dinner was much

lighter. Once they were done, Ms. Edie showed him around.

"There's a bathroom down here, so no need to come up and down those creaky stairs at night," the older woman said.

Duncan eyed the phone booth sized shower. He'd have to clean one half of his body at a time. "Looks perfect."

"As I said, I only have one other bed in this house so, you'll have to sleep on the couch, Duncan."

He made eye contact with Retta who mouthed, "I'm sorry."

This was shaping up to be as cozy as the time he regrettably went camping with one of his friends in high school.

"My toaster oven, blender, and crockpot are off-limits to you," Ms. Edie said, pointing to him.

"The toaster, really?" Retta said. "What would you have him do? Starve?"

"If that would keep him from touching my appliances, sure."

Duncan was delightfully taken aback at the old woman's words.

"She's joking," Retta said, turning to him.

"No, I would've laughed otherwise," Ms. Edie said as they walked into the living room.

They all studied the dark green sofa that, to its credit, looked incredibly plush. But there was no way his feet weren't hanging off the edge.

"Your back is going to kill you," Ms. Edie said matter of factly. She provided no alternative solution or consoling gesture.

"Again, the walls are thin, the stairs are creaky, so please don't try anything. I like my eight hours," the woman said.

They left him downstairs, and he got ready for bed, trying not to disturb anything in the bathroom too much. Once Duncan settled into his couch for the night, he couldn't shake the unsettling feeling that someone was watching him. It wasn't until he sat up and flicked on the lamp near him that he found Ms. Edie's cat perched on the settee on the other side of the living room.

He tried a few times to shoo the feline away, but she sat there watching him. Eventually, he grew tired of staring down the cat, and he accepted the possibility he might wake up in a pool of his own blood.

———

Waking up in her grandmother's pristine guest room made Retta want to sink deeper into the bed. This was the only place where she could sleep in. She hadn't been here in almost a year, and the last time she was, she'd been in the middle of a spiral over her *Winner Bakes All* "win" and recent breakup.

Not wanting to tarnish the moment, Retta got up and ready for the day. From experience, she knew her granny would've already eaten, but a box of cereal and a pot of tepid coffee would be waiting for her.

As she descended the stairs, she spotted Duncan and her grandmother sitting at the breakfast nook, silent. Retta loved that the older woman was able to knock Duncan down a few pegs. He thought he'd come in here with his smile and strong shoulders and charm Grandma Edie, ha!

"Good morning," she said.

Duncan turned around and winked at her.

Her gran moved the newspaper from in front of her face long enough to reveal her bob with blunt bangs and say, "Morning, sweetheart. The cereal box is on the counter."

After preparing her breakfast, Retta joined Duncan and her grandmother at the table.

"How was everyone's night?" she asked, breaking the silence.

"Perfectly fine," her granny replied.

Duncan closed his eyes and shook his head.

Pressing her lips together she dumped teaspoons of sugar into her coffee and doused it with almond milk to make it somewhat palatable.

"I should get you better coffee, granny."

"I've been drinking that brand for thirty years. It hasn't killed me yet."

"That's a low bar. You should want it to taste good," Retta said as she gathered a spoonful of cereal.

"The best coffee I've had is from that cafe we first met at," Duncan said.

"I haven't actually tried—"

Her grandmother tsked behind the newspaper.

Retta looked sideways at Duncan. "Is everything okay?"

She didn't answer right away, and when she did, it was from behind the paper. "Well, last night you told me you met because your businesses are beside each other, but now you're saying you met at some coffee shop." She dropped the newspaper. "What is the truth?"

"Both are true. We briefly met at the coffee shop before officially meeting when we realized we were neighbors," Retta said.

Her grandmother pursed her lips and studied the two of them before saying to Duncan, "You seem like the flighty type. I don't know if I trust you."

It could be intimidating being on the receiving end of

Edith Rankine's sharp tongue, but before Retta could smoothly change the subject, Duncan said, "That's cool. I'm grateful you let me stay here, but at the end of the day, I'm here for Retta."

His words made her tingly all over. She knew he meant he was there because of their agreement, but for a moment it sounded as if he was truly there for her and not parking spaces.

Her grandmother made a non-decipherable sound before returning to her reading material.

"I think I'll go for a run," Duncan said, getting up from his seat. "Excuse me."

When he disappeared into the bathroom, Retta said, "You're doing too much."

"Perhaps," her grandmother replied.

"He's a good guy."

"We thought that of the last one as well," the older woman said.

Retta shook her head. Sure, Chris was sometimes condescending and she'd mistaken his arrogance for wit, but he wasn't a bad guy. She even suspected she would've thought fondly of their relationship if they'd had a regular breakup.

"Get to know him."

"Why?" the older woman asked, without looking up from her page. "So, I can see all the ways you're too good for him?"

Retta's heart squeezed. Her grandmother had been there for her during her breakup and career setback. She'd escaped to this mountainous small town to hide away for several weeks, and her tough as nails granny let her. Not only that, but Grandma Edie had also cooked her a huge batch of beef stew with tons of garlic and chilies and cut her sarcastic comments in half.

They both remained quiet as Duncan emerged from the bathroom in running shorts, shoes, and a t-shirt.

"All right, I'm heading out," he said.

Retta turned to wave, trying not to sigh at the image he cut in his workout clothes.

Once he'd left the house, Retta said, "He's a good one. Trust me."

She hated that it was important to her that her grandmother liked and approved of her fake boyfriend.

Her granny scoffed and collected her smart speaker before moving to the balcony with Levi right behind her. "We'll see."

———

When Duncan returned from his run, Ms. Edie asked if he wanted to help her in the garden. Actually, she more or less told him he was assisting her.

"You think I'm safe?" he asked Retta, whispering from the side of his mouth.

"You'll be fine," Retta said, blowing a curl out of her face. She was in full-blown baking mode with an apron fastened around her waist and hands covered in dough. "As long as you don't bring up her ex-husbands. Or the unfinished patio."

"No exes or renos. Got it."

Exiting the house, he was met with birdsong and Levi with a ball in his mouth. Duncan chucked the toy across the manicured yard and watched the good boy run to retrieve it, his dark coat gleaming under the sun.

"I'd like to get this done before the Second Coming if that's fine with you," Ms. Edie called out to him without turning around. She knelt in front of a small garden bed near the right side of her property. The wide-brimmed hat she wore completely hid her face.

"Pull the grass you see poking out through the soil," she said when he joined her. "Make sure you don't disturb the vegetables."

They worked side-by-side mostly in silence. She picked beautiful ripe tomatoes while Duncan split his time playing with Levi and pulling grass and weeds.

"My granddaughter wants me to get to know you," Ms. Edie said after several minutes. She pushed her large hat back and peered over her sunglasses at him. "Are you worth knowing?"

"Yes?" Duncan replied.

"You don't sound so sure."

He wasn't. Half of his brain was thinking about how he wouldn't see the older woman ever again after this weekend. Getting to know him would be a waste of her time.

Before he could respond, she winced and shook her hand for several seconds.

"You okay?" Duncan asked.

"Of course," she said, going back to picking tomatoes. "And don't you go worrying Coretta about anything. It's carpal tunnel. An occupational hazard of doing hair for fifty years."

"If you want, I can show you some exercises that might help," Duncan said.

The older woman stilled before pushing her hat back once again to look at him. "I can't stop you."

Duncan smiled. That was as big of a resounding yes as he was going to get. He sat on the grass and Ms. Edie followed suit, discarding her gardening gloves and tools.

He started with a simple stretch that she mimicked. "Stop if you feel any discomfort," he said.

They worked through several exercises, and after a few minutes she asked, "What are your intentions with her?"

Intentions? Duncan didn't know what she wanted him to say, but he knew he couldn't lie. Mainly because Ms. Edie would call bullshit.

"I care for Retta," Duncan said. "I want to be there for her and make her happy."

Even behind the sunglasses, he could feel her scrutinizing stare.

"Good," she finally said. "She's been hurt before, and she deserves someone dependable because she throws herself fully into everything she does."

Duncan nodded. He couldn't be that guy, but he wholeheartedly agreed Retta deserved the best.

"When she and her brother were younger, they'd come down here for winter breaks," Ms. Edie said, pausing for a moment to pet Levi who'd taken to lying beside her. "We took them skating on the lake one year. They'd both never done it before. Her brother gave up once he fell a few times, but she spent hours that day trying to get the hang of it."

"Did she?" Duncan asked.

"Oh yes, she was able to skate around the lake once without falling. That's the kind of commitment she deserves."

Something tightened in Duncan's chest.

He was about to say something when the topic of their conversation stepped out of the house, carrying two glasses of punch. She looked charming in her apron covered in flour and her unruly coils.

Duncan moved to get up, but Retta said, "No, stay. I'll join you. I thought you two could use something to drink."

She handed him and Ms. Edie each a glass before taking a seat in the grass with them.

The older woman took a sip and said, "Thank you, love."

"It's good," Duncan said as he lightly smacked his lips in response to the tangy cranberry flavor. "Thank you." Without so much as a second thought, he leaned in and kissed the side of her face.

He wished he could say the move was part of his performance as her boyfriend, but it came too naturally.

"You're all sweaty," Retta said, smiling and dramatically wiping her face with her apron.

He teasingly went in for a hug. "Come on, it's only a little perspiration."

Giggling, Retta ducked to avoid him. He then grabbed her ankle and attempted to pull her toward him.

"Is this my punishment for not letting you share a bed?" Ms. Edie asked, watching them over her sunglasses.

They both froze.

Retta scooted out of his reach and cleared her throat before saying, "The sour cherry pies are done. All I have to do is put them in the oven before we eat dinner."

"I'm excited to try it," Duncan said.

"Not to brag or anything, but the recipe won me the final mini-challenge on *Winner Bakes All*."

"Nice—"

"You told him about the show?" Ms. Edie asked, her thin eyebrows high on her face.

"Yeah, it came up," Retta said, playing with blades of grass.

"Hm," Ms. Edie said before turning to Duncan. "I guess you are worth knowing after all."

Chapter Seventeen

IT WAS STILL dark outside when Retta's alarm went off. Whenever she visited her grandmother, she was compelled to watch the sunrise at least once. She'd never been someone who was awed by nature until she'd experienced a Cedar Lake sunrise as a teen. A rendering of it was submitted for her high school senior art project.

After getting ready, she did her best to descend the stairs and not hit the squeaky points. She had no gripes about going alone or with Levi, she actually preferred it, but she also knew Duncan slept in the living room and might appreciate an invitation.

She felt her way into the living room, almost tripping over a dog toy. Squinting, she cautiously approached Duncan. He'd somehow pretzeled himself onto the couch, and it didn't look remotely comfortable.

"Duncan," she whispered.

Not so much as a twitch.

She got nearer and said his name again.

Nothing.

Time was of the essence; the sun waited for nobody.

Retta pressed her hand on his shoulder and gently jostled him, and before she could register what was happening, Duncan grabbed her wrist.

She croaked. "Yeah, okay, that's a bit tight," she said, patting his shoulder to get him to release her.

"What are you doing here?" he whispered as he loosened his grip but didn't let go.

"I-I'm driving out to one of the mountains to watch the sunrise, and I was wondering if you wanted to join me? You don't have to."

"Right now?" he asked, his voice rough with sleep.

Retta looked down at her phone, the light breaking the darkness. Sunrise would begin at 5:25, and it took about thirty minutes to get to their destination.

"Yeah."

He swung his legs over onto the floor, but he sat there for a while making circles on the palm of her hand with his thumb. How could a simple caress make it hard to draw a breath?

"Duncan?"

"Sorry, I'm trying to wake up," he said as he brought her wrist to his lips and kissed it. "Please, make yourself comfortable." He gestured toward his makeshift bed once he got up and collected his duffle bag.

She was left standing in the dark, listening to the drone of the bathroom fan and running water. During those minutes she decided to use the soft light of the disappearing moon to retrieve a few blankets and make tea to take along on their trip.

By the time Duncan emerged from the washroom, she had everything prepared.

"Let's get a look at this sunrise then," he said.

———

Duncan was glad Retta had suggested they take his large pick-up truck because he didn't think her small car would've made it through the bumpy road during the last fifteen minutes of the journey. It was the type of rough terrain where he was sure they'd arrive with their teeth in their laps. Mercifully, they got to the top of the mountain with no dental emergencies.

They parked in a clearing the size of a basketball court, bracketed off by small trees and shrubs. It provided them with the perfect view of the still-sleeping town below.

"That's Cedar Lake," Retta said, pointing to the body of water far in the distance to their left.

As the gray sky lightened, they created a comfortable cocoon outside in the back of the pick-up with blankets Retta had had the foresight to bring.

Climbing up the tailgate, he settled on the rear panel of the truck, and when Retta joined him with a thermos and cups, he hauled her against him.

"I can't believe you have me out here in the dark waiting for the sun," he said.

She handed him his mug filled with tea. "I promise it's worth it. Especially since we're indoors all day tomorrow at the wedding."

They'd been working toward this event, and as they sat there in the dusk, he wondered how she was handling her ex's impending marriage. He shouldn't care, but he did.

"How are you feeling about tomorrow, anyway?"

She looked at him. "Good. Why? Are you having second thoughts?"

"No," he said, quickly. "Nothing like that. I'm... I was wondering if you're accomplishing what you set out with this whole plan."

"I think so," she said, laughing. "It's kinda funny how

this is all a self-made problem I could get rid of by not caring."

It was beyond Duncan what she saw in her ex. She was going through all of this for a man who was dull, uncharismatic, and entirely too—

"It's time," Retta said, straightening against him.

The previously gray sky brightened before it burst into magenta and coral as the sun slowly emerged from behind the mountains. It brushed the town below in its glow. And downy clouds tinged purple drifted by with silhouetted birds close behind. The whole scene looked like it had been computer-generated.

Duncan pulled out his phone to take a photo, but he soon realized it didn't capture the essence of what he was viewing. "I get it."

She sighed. "Right?"

He looked at her as she watched the scene. The light cast its warm hues on her face, and he had an urge, yet again, to capture beauty with a picture. Instead, he lowered his head and nibbled on the tip of her ear.

"Look at the fucking view," she said, squirming under his touch.

Looking at her, he said, "I am."

She rolled her eyes. "Pfft. I know you can do better than that corny ass line."

He laughed against her scarf covered head as a feeling he couldn't really identify settled in his body. The contents of his chest wanted to break free.

Refusing to interrogate it right then and there, he nuzzled Retta's neck, taking in the light vanilla scent of her body lotion.

When she turned to look at him, he thought she might repeat her request for him to watch the sunrise, but she kissed him instead. Her tongue was still warm from the tea.

With her right arm, she reached up and around and closed her fist around his hair. "Touch me."

Her desired destination for him was made clear when she widened her legs.

"Is this why you invited me?" he asked as he moved his hand to the waistband of her leggings. "Was the sunrise an excuse for me to play with this pretty pussy?"

She didn't answer as his hand followed the strip of trimmed hair toward her clit. Her breath faltered, and she leaned back into him. Less than a minute into stroking and rubbing her, his fingers were coated with her wetness.

"You're trying to kill me," she said when he stopped his teasing circles around her clit to spread her legs wider.

He kissed her temple. "Never."

"Tell me you have a condom," she said, fondling the front of his pants.

Reaching into his wallet, he retrieved the square packet before he lowered his track pants and rolled the latex onto his already hard dick.

"All yours," he said as he watched her drop her own pants and straddle him. He wanted to feel her bare body against him, but they were already too far gone.

She cupped his face in her hands as she lowered onto his dick, and he forced himself to savor it. Take in every detail. They both moaned into each other's mouths as she settled herself fully on him.

Her glasses sat precariously on her nose as she stilled and got comfortable with him inside her like this. When she finally started moving, he grabbed her hips and kept her upright. She found a rhythm that was torturously slow, but he was sustained by her little open mouth gasps and the way her eyes rolled back into her head every time she came down to the hilt.

He wanted to extend this moment.

Halfway through an upward stroke, she breathlessly said, "Help me go faster."

Drawing her forehead to his, he met her next downward movement with a thrust.

"Duncan," she yelped, leaning forward to hold onto the vehicle's structure.

"Is this what your pussy needs?" he asked, meeting her once again with a powerful drive upward. "It's all fucking yours, Retta. Every inch of it."

While their bodies connected and produced crude, raw noises, he realized he'd have to go back to his real life soon. How did he do that when he knew what it felt like to be with her, to hear his name on her lips? He pushed the thoughts out of his mind. All he could do at this point was give her the most of this fucking.

"God, I'm coming" she whimpered, putting two of her fingers into his mouth before pressing them to her clit. She rubbed herself and continued to bounce up and down on his dick until a scream left her parted lips.

Her firm tug on his hair spurred him to hold her in place as he drove into her slick pussy in search of his own ecstasy.

Their gazes locked, and she said, "Come for me."

He stilled as a shuddering orgasm hit and had him seeing more vibrant colors than he'd witnessed in the sky.

———

After their morning on the mountain, the rest of the day had been spent lounging around the house and in the backyard, but at around six in the afternoon, Retta suggested they prepare a meal. That's how Duncan found himself arranging vegetables picked from Ms. Edie's garden onto wooden skewers. Ms. Edie excluded herself from the process and was instead completing a Sudoku puzzle on her tablet at the kitchen counter.

"Don't make them too big, Coretta."

Duncan laughed at the exasperated look on Retta's face as she adjusted the size of her zucchini slices. This all felt comfortably domestic.

"You ready for the wedding? Everything ironed out and pressed? You know how they are," Ms. Edie said.

Retta shook her head, catching his questioning look. "She's under the impression that my dad's side of the family is snobbish."

"They are," the older woman said. "I'm sorry I don't know the different regions that make wine. And if I have to sprain my tongue to pronounce an alcoholic drink, is it really worth it?"

"Is that why you're not coming to the wedding?" Duncan asked, smiling.

Ms. Edie put down her tablet. "Well, that and the fact the groom is—"

Retta coughed and banged the counter.

He looked between the women as they communicated with their eyes.

"What exactly happens at weddings?" he asked, taking that as a cue to change subjects.

"You've never been to one?" Retta asked.

"I've seen it in movies, and I went to a few as a kid."

Retta dumped another heap of vegetables in front of him. "Oh, it's basically drunk dancing to Top 40 hits till early in the morning."

"So, a good time?" he asked.

"If people could stop pulling out their phones on the dance floor, it could be. Nobody wants to see themselves all over social media mid-twerk, sweaty, and tipsy."

He smiled at her. "Are you speaking from experience?"

"Yes, and now all I do at weddings are the line dances."

"Don't forget the long-winded speeches," Ms. Edie said. "Every single one I've heard can be shortened. Your Vegas trip isn't special."

Duncan laughed thinking about the brutal process he'd been through trying to formulate a speech these last few weeks. "I'll have to hire you to look over mine then."

"What's it for? Wedding? Bar mitzvah? Retirement?" Ms. Edie asked, counting off the options on her hand. "I'll tell you exactly what you need to say."

"My parent's divorce party."

Ms. Edie blinked at him for several seconds. "I'm sorry. Did you say divorce *party*?"

"Granny," Retta said. Her tone had a subtle warning.

He nodded and couldn't stop smiling as the older woman stood up, grabbed her tablet and coffee mug, and walked out of the room.

Sighing, Retta went on to finish chopping the vegetables with skillful precision.

When she moved over to his area to expedite the skewering, she asked, "So your parents are still going through with it? The divorce, I mean."

"That's what they're saying."

"And how's your speech?" Retta asked.

"A delicate balance between the truth and what people want to hear."

"If my grandmother was still in the room, she'd tell you not to mince your words."

"There's no way I'm speaking from the heart at this thing," he said.

"Oh, I get it. I mince my words all the time. That's why I aggressively journal," she said before snapping her fingers. "Now, there's an idea. You should write an unfiltered version of your speech that you won't show anyone.

That way you can vent without hurting people's feelings."

It couldn't be any more painful than coming up with multiple synonyms for the same word.

"I'll give it a try."

Chapter Eighteen

IT WAS the morning of the wedding, and Retta got ready with a knot in the pit of her stomach like it might be her walking down the aisle. All the breathing and affirming words weren't helping the anxiety coursing through her body.

If she were honest, she would admit her nerves were not only about the day ahead. Yesterday, while watching the sunrise with Duncan, she'd been plagued with the feeling of wanting to stop time.

She gave the dress she'd picked out with Nia's help a final tug before pushing down her turbulent thoughts and heading downstairs.

"Now hold it," Duncan said before Retta entered the room.

When she rounded the corner, she found her grandmother in a fuchsia tracksuit with short spikey maroon hair, performing a one-legged squat. Duncan stood beside her in his suit, positioned to prevent any mishaps.

"Oh my God," Retta said when her grandmother

straightened and laughed. That particular sound surfaced as often as a lunar eclipse.

"Coretta," her grandmother said. "You see this?" She proceeded to repeat the move without hesitation.

"Incredible," Retta responded, shaking her head.

Directing her gaze toward Duncan, she found him already looking at her. Her stomach did a somersault, and she swallowed hard.

"You look beautiful," he said. There were several feet separating them, but he might as well have whispered the words right into her ear.

Her grandmother walked over to her, examining the material and holding her at arm's-length. "I agree. Come, Duncan. I'll take a picture before you two go."

"Let me quickly tie my tie," he said, moving to the bathroom.

"He's a nice boy," her grandmother said after he'd left the room.

Retta nodded, sipping the tea she'd poured. She'd opted out of being smug about the change of opinion.

"Now I can see why you love him."

Hot liquid sloshed over the edge of Retta's mug. "Crap." She moved toward the sink to run her hand under cold water.

"Am I wrong?" her grandmother asked, handing Retta a rag to dry with.

"Yes, it's very early."

Among other things.

The older woman made a contemplative sound as she grabbed a bowl from the cupboard. Thankfully, the conversation was dropped when Duncan exited the bathroom.

It was showtime.

———

Retta drove them over to the church. Duncan didn't try to fill the silence, sensing she might need time to mentally prepare. Once they arrived, he assumed his role as boyfriend and took her hand in his.

"You ready?" he whispered, kissing the back of her hand.

She nodded and smiled at him as they entered the church. The foyer was bustling with perfectly dressed children who ran around and adults in vibrant colored outfits.

"Coretta! Look at you, my darling," a woman with a pink dress and a matching hat said from across the foyer. She came over to hug Retta.

"Auntie, this is Duncan. Baby, this is my Aunt Cynthia."

"Nice to meet you, ma'am," Duncan said, giving the woman his biggest, brightest smile.

"Oh, Retta," the woman said, looking between the two of them. She drew close to her niece and whispered something in her ear.

Retta laughed, monotone and airy. Nothing like her natural squeaky cackle.

When the older woman departed Retta leaned in toward him and said, "She thinks you're handsome, but my dress is too short apparently."

Duncan looked at her green outfit that popped against her brown skin. Her long legs extended forever past the hem. "I disagree."

She squeezed his hand in response.

"But I will say," he lowered his voice, "I've already pictured you bent over in this dress."

Retta didn't even look at him. She simply dropped her head and brought a finger to her ear like she had a Bluetooth earpiece on. "Mhmm. Beelzebub? Yeah, I have a twenty-nine-year-old male for you."

He threw his head back and laughed. She was definitely more relaxed than she had been at the engagement party.

As they continued to walk around the foyer, they stopped once in a while for Retta to introduce him to more of her family.

"The man approaching us in the red tie is my Uncle Seth," she whispered and turned her head so her mouth wasn't visible. "He refuses to remember what anyone in the family under the age of forty does for a living. He assumes we're all still in school."

"Hi, Uncle," Retta said, turning back around and smiling at the stocky man with thin glasses.

"Oh, Coretta, I haven't seen you in a while. How's school going?"

Duncan smiled.

Retta shrugged and steered him into a brief conversation about some sporting game before they exited that conversation as well.

Mrs. Majors appeared from somewhere in the crowd and advanced toward them. "When did you get here?"

"A few minutes ago," Retta said to her mother.

Mrs. Majors looked at him. "It's nice to see you again, Duncan. You'll need to come to dinner soon so we can actually have a proper conversation."

"I'll have to look at my schedule," he said, feeling a bit bad about the fact that he already knew there wouldn't be a dinner.

Satisfied with his response, Mrs. Majors squeezed both their arms and left to talk to others.

Meanwhile, the two of them headed to the auditorium to grab their seats.

"Left is for the bride, the right side is for the groom," an usher said as he handed them programs in the shape of fans and two vials of what Retta told him was bubble solution.

"For after the ceremony when they walk out of the church," she elaborated.

Immediately inside the sanctuary, there was a large framed photo of Irene and Chris that Retta stopped to study.

Duncan wished he was a mind reader. "You okay?"

"Yeah, I'm fine," she said, immediately abandoning the photograph to move deeper into the church.

As they settled into a pew, Retta's knee started bouncing with no evidence of slowing down.

He playfully squeezed her thigh and eyed her shoe with the aggressive heel. "You're going to make a hole in the floorboards."

She smiled and crossed her legs, trapping his hand. But even the little flirting couldn't distract him from how long everything was taking. He kept looking at his phone; they were twenty minutes behind schedule. Sweat was starting to build around his torso, and he now knew why the programs were fashioned into fans. The church had no central air conditioning. He waved the fan back and forth, making sure he got Retta as well.

"What time are these things supposed to start?" he asked not too quietly.

"Baby, this is a Black wedding. We're early," the woman sitting beside them said.

After several minutes, Retta's mother snuck toward them from the front of the church, waving at people but definitely on a mission.

"Sweetheart, could you run this to Irene," her mother

asked, holding out a pair of earrings. "I can ask someone else if—"

"She's here?" Retta asked, frowning.

"Yeah. They had a whole mix up at the hotel about check out time, so she's finishing her preparation in the church's nursery."

"I'll be back," Retta said to him, scooting out of the pew. He watched her exit the auditorium, wishing he could escape too.

The woman seated next to him tapped his shoulder. "Here," she said, holding out a wrapped hard candy. "To pass the time."

———

As Retta walked through the halls of the church, she greeted the people she recognized. The farther she walked, however, the quieter it became. None of the doors were labeled, so she knocked on each one before entering.

"Irene?" she called into a vacant, dark space that held extra chairs and tables.

In another room she found the harpist tuning her instrument for the ceremony. Retta marveled at how big the instrument was in person.

The musician looked her way, and Retta backed out apologetically. "It's beautiful," she said as she closed the door behind her.

When she arrived at the last room, she hoped it was the correct one. It was much too hot to be speed walking through the hallway like she was.

She knocked and peeked inside but only found an empty nursery. Instead of immediately heading back to the auditorium, she exited the building through the back entrance, hoping to catch a breeze. She stepped outside and found stagnant air and a small field, unkempt with overgrown grass and an abandoned pew.

Retta moved to return indoors and report back to her mother when she spotted something white move in her peripheral vision.

Her cousin was standing against the side of the building vaping in her poofy wedding dress.

"I've been looking for you," Retta said as she approached Irene.

"I'm here," her cousin replied brightly, but it wasn't until Irene sniffled and ran her fingers underneath her eyes that Retta recognized her cousin had been crying.

"What's wrong?" she asked.

"Nothing," Irene said, laughing but her laugh got cut off by a gulp that involuntarily turned into a sob.

"Oh my God," Retta said as she neared and awkwardly patted her cousin's back.

When Irene's tears subsided, she looked up. Her makeup was slightly smudged, and her eyelashes definitely would need to be glued down again before she walked down the aisle, but as usual, she looked great.

"I'm sorry," Irene said, taking another inhale from her vape. "It's the nerves, you know?"

"Of course," Retta replied, withdrawing her comforting hand. "It's okay."

Irene nodded, gazing into the shabby field.

Remembering her assignment, Retta produced the dainty hooped earrings. "I was told to give you these."

Irene looked at the accessories but made no move to grab them. Instead, she said, "I like your dress."

Retta pushed up her glasses. "Thanks. I like yours too."

They both laughed a little bit before Retta once again held out her hand with the earrings and said, "All right. I'm going to head on inside—"

"Is this weird for you?" Irene asked, blowing a big puff of smoke into the air from the corner of her mouth. "Being here?"

Maybe it was the fact her charade with Duncan was winding down, but Retta stopped short of responding with her usual pacifying answer. "Yes."

"Why did you come?" Irene asked.

Shrugging, Retta said, "Because people expected me not to."

"So, you're trying to prove something?"

"Yeah, that this"—She gestured around them —"doesn't bother me."

"But it does," her cousin said.

Retta had spent a year saying none of *this* fazed her, acting cool and collected as her ex's new relationship played out in front of her. But she'd had a lot of feelings.

"Can I ask you something?"

Irene paused with her vape pen in her mouth. "Sure."

"Why him?" Retta briefly questioned the wisdom of broaching this overdue conversation at this moment. "Out of everyone on this damned planet, why him?"

It had been salt in the wound, no, a gut-punch when she'd been confronted with Chris and Irene's relationship on social media a month after her breakup. She'd literally chucked her phone across the room when she saw the picture of them smiling in each other's embrace. There'd been a lot cussing, some rageful prayer, and an emergency friend hangout with Nia and Kym.

Irene sniffled and avoided eye contact. "I didn't do it to hurt you. Chris is so impressive and accomplished, and I was drawn to that after years of dating guys who didn't keep stable jobs and couldn't bother to remember my birthday. If it could've been anyone else…"

Retta nodded, looking up to the sky and blinking

rapidly. She'd bottled up her anger, disappointment, and hurt for so long.

That approach had stalled her emotional recovery in service of not giving people any more reason to pity her. Her pride had been on the line.

When Retta finally got a grip on her tears, she found her cousin watching her.

"I'm sorry," Irene said.

"It's fine." Retta shook her head. "That's a lie. I was pissed. It felt like a betrayal, and it was embarrassing having everyone trying to figure out what flaws made Chris dump me for you."

While they stood in silence, staring at the untidy bush in front of them, something from Retta's soul released. Her admittance made her lighter.

"But if I'm being honest, you and him are more compatible," Retta said. This was her olive branch. She didn't want to spend the next decades avoiding her cousin and building resentment over a guy she didn't even have feelings for anymore. "Country clubs and fancy events have never been my scene."

Irene laughed, wryly. "They get old fast."

"Yeah, they do, don't they?" Retta said smiling as she produced the earrings she'd been sent to deliver. "This has been an unexpected but nice conversation—"

"I never dreamed about my wedding day until I was planning this one," Irene said.

"I don't think that's unusual," Retta replied, dropping her outstretched arm.

"But I also have this feeling that this will be the last interesting thing I do with my life."

Retta frowned. "That's not true. You have plenty to look forward to. You still do pageants, right?"

"I stopped two years ago."

"Well, you're still young."

"I'm almost thirty," her cousin said.

She was twenty-four.

"Even so, you have time," Retta said.

"Perhaps, or maybe I'll forever be known as Chris's wife who placed third in a national pageant one time," Irene said, taking a long drag from her vape pen. "And when I hit my middle ages at thirty-five, I'll have to do something like run a marathon to feel alive. I fucking hate running."

"Okay, well, firstly midlife starts a little later—"

"But if I needed to run, I could. It's just one foot in front of the other…"

Her cousin was mostly talking to herself now, hence the senseless words coming out of her mouth. Before Retta could finally extricate herself, Irene looked at her with wide eyes. It was like the sun had come out.

"You good?" Retta asked.

Instead of answering, Irene pulled out her phone and rapidly moved her fingers across the keyboard. When she stopped after a minute, she said, "I need you to do something for me. Tell Chris and my mom I'm sorry."

"Sorry for what?"

"Leaving," she said as she picked up her purse and started running as fast as her heels and big dress would allow toward the front of the church.

"Wait," Retta shouted, hobbling after her. "Where are you going?"

Her cousin turned long enough in the flurry of white tulle to say, "I can't marry Chris right now."

"I-I don't understand?"

Irene's attention was pulled by a message that arrived on her phone with a ping. "I have to go."

"You're not getting married?" she asked, her heart pounding as she advanced toward her cousin.

"No."

"Okay, okay," Retta said, finding it hard to formulate words. "That's fine. We'll walk in together, and you can tell your mom."

But Irene was backing away shaking her head. "I can't. I'm sorry."

"Wait—"

But Irene was off, running through the parking lot, dropping her vape pen along the way. Retta tried to catch up, but she stopped when she spotted the yellow cab in the church lot. Her cousin entered the car, barely pulling in all the material that made up her dress before shutting the door. The cab drove off, and just like that, Retta was left in horrified silence.

No one was out there. The attendees were probably sitting in the auditorium waiting for the festivities to begin. She had to tell someone. Who did she tell? God, what if she had to announce it to everyone. Retta furiously fanned herself with the wedding program until a strong grip encircled her upper arm.

"Retta," Duncan said. "What's wrong?"

She might throw up.

"Look at me. Look at me," he said. "Baby—"

"Irene left."

Duncan frowned. "What do you mean she left?"

"I mean she's a fucking runaway bride," Retta said, looking down at her hand where she still held her cousin's earrings. "I found her crying. We talked. It was actually a really good conversation. Therapeutic and what not. Then she said she wasn't down with this whole marriage thing and left."

Duncan held her on either side of her face. "I'm going to grab your mother."

He disappeared into the auditorium and shortly returned with her mom.

"What's going on?"

Retta retold the sequence of events as fast as she could.

"Oh, dear God," her mom said before moving into action and heading into the main part of the church.

Duncan grabbed her hand, and they followed, stopping right behind the pew closest to the door. There was no need to take a seat.

"This is so bad," Retta whispered as she watched an uncomfortable version of "Telephone" unfold where her mother whispered into the wedding planner's ear who then walked over to Irene's mom. All three of them then approached Mrs. Washington, who then went up to her son to deliver the news.

The auditorium held a stable hum of chatter, but the noise increased as people sensed something was off.

Meanwhile, Retta knew she would've keeled over from the anxiety of watching all of this go down if Duncan hadn't been holding her. She appreciated the comforting circles he was making on her arm.

Chris might be her ex, but watching his face drop when his mother told him the news was something she couldn't find glee in. She knew what it felt like not to be chosen. And it sucked.

Moments later, he stepped front and center on the church stage. Everyone fell silent save for a baby who wailed like she knew what was coming.

"There will be no wedding today," Chris said, his voice booming through the sanctuary.

There was a collective gasp and a beat of silence before fevered conversation commenced. Stepping off the platform, Chris strode out of the auditorium with his mother and a few other relatives in tow. As he passed them, Retta's hand automatically reached out, but he was too far away and too focused on his exit to have noticed.

As the pastor of the church approached the microphone, Retta turned to Duncan and said, "We need to go."

———

Duncan and Ms. Edie sat next to each other and across from Retta at the dining table. They'd broken down what had happened at the wedding to the older woman, but now they were in a meditative portion of the conversation where Retta would once in a while say, "I can't believe it" and take a sip of her tea.

However, Duncan could believe it. And both Irene and Chris should consider themselves lucky that it happened now and not several kids and thousands of fights later.

"If you ask me, he got what was coming to him," Ms. Edie said.

"Granny, not now."

The light admonishment made something twist in Duncan's stomach. Retta had reached for Chris as he'd stormed out of the church. She felt protective of him despite who he'd planned to marry. That much was clear.

Ms. Edie let out a long-suffering sigh. "Well, okay, then. What's the plan? Are you two leaving tomorrow or heading back today?"

"I'm cool leaving tomorrow morning," Retta said, looking at him for confirmation. "There's no point in rushing out of here now."

Duncan nodded. "That works for me." He might be sleeping in the smallest bed imaginable and surveilled by a cat all through the night, but there was something comforting about being in this house.

"I'd planned to order pizza while you were at the wedding, so if you want any, you'll have to pitch in," Ms. Edie said.

"I can throw together some cocktails to make it a real party," Duncan said.

Ms. Edie pointed to him with her thumb and spoke to Retta. "I love this boy."

Her granddaughter smiled and rolled her eyes.

"All right, I'm going to take Levi out for a walk," the older woman said.

In the meantime, Duncan and Retta cleared the remnants of their lunch. He then moved to his makeshift bedroom to get some clothes he could change into.

When he entered the kitchen, he found Retta leaning over the counter, studying her phone. The pretty dress she wore paired with the house slippers were oddly adorable.

"Look," Retta said, holding up her phone. "We're adding Earl Grey éclairs to our fall menu. Omar sent me some of the photos he took for the website."

Duncan drew closer and looked at the stylistic over-head photos of the oblong dessert. "It looks really good."

Retta smiled and examined the photo again. "On Monday I'll bring some over."

He froze. They hadn't discussed anything about how they would interact after their "relationship" ended. It was expected that they'd remain friendly. But as he changed out of his suit in the bathroom, panic wanted to claw its way through him as the truth became clear. He'd grown attached.

Their bargain had technically been fulfilled regardless of the disastrous wedding. Right now he should be doing everything in his power to get back to his real life where he was single, but he *wanted* to stay.

Leaving the bathroom, he wasn't sure what he was going to do until he started packing his bags and reorganizing the living room. It was necessary for him to leave now.

Retta walked into the room then with a glass of water. "Do you want to watch a movie? I have—"

She looked at the duffle bag slung across his chest.

"Where're you going?" she asked.

He coughed to clear his throat. "I think I should go."

"I thought we'd decided to leave tomorrow."

"Yeah, then I realized I could make it back before sunset and actually sleep in a bed tonight."

Something compressed in his chest as he watched her eyes dim a little.

Her features straightened as she said, "You're right. There's no reason for you to stay."

The conversation was operating on two levels, and he had the impression this was their breakup. When he spoke next it was a wonder his voice didn't falter. "Thank your grandmother for me."

He refused to look at Retta as he left the house. While walking to his parked car across the street, he spotted Ms. Edie round the bend with Levi.

Changing his destination, he approached the old lady who'd stopped to study him.

"I'm leaving."

You mean running.

She looked at his jacket and bag. "I see that."

"I want to thank you for your hospitality and—"

"Better get going then. Don't want to hit traffic."

It was a weekend; there'd be no traffic.

Though he thought he was making the right move, the

farther away he drove from Ms. Edie's home, the harder it was to shake off the dull ache in the middle of his chest.

———————

Retta stood looking at the front door that Duncan had left through. She felt heat, so much heat on her face and her body. She wanted to step out of her skin, leaving it behind to crawl into a corner.

Retreating upstairs, she peeled the silly dress from her body and scrubbed her face of the suddenly garish makeup. She found herself here, embarrassed and pining, because she hadn't made a big enough effort to distinguish the fake from the real. In the back of her mind, she'd foolishly hoped they'd continue like this.

Armed with a 1000 piece puzzle she'd found on a shelf in the bedroom, Retta walked downstairs ready to distract herself all evening. She was surprised to find her grandmother in front of the stove.

"I thought we were ordering pizza," Retta said, coming over to stand beside the older woman and look into the pot where she was browning onions and garlic.

"I don't know. I felt beef stew would be more appropriate today."

It was then that Retta's tears had no other choice but to fall.

Chapter Nineteen

THERE'S a moment in the middle of an activity you're doing for the first time when you realize it is harder than you expected.

Duncan reread the instructions for the blueberry scones with lemon glaze for the third time and looked back at the soupy mess he had in his bowl. There was no reason why he shouldn't have perfectly pliable dough at this point.

Grabbing the hefty bag of flour, he added more of the powder to the mixture. While combining the extra ingredient, the buzzer to his apartment rang.

He'd been expecting Anthony to come through with some documents that needed signing, but when his friend stepped into his apartment he had nothing with him.

"How are you?" Anthony asked, reducing the volume on the TV before taking a seat on one of the stools at the kitchen counter.

Duncan looked up from where he'd dropped the more solid dough onto the counter to roll. "Fine?"

"Yeah?"

"Yeah," Duncan said, as he rummaged through his cupboard for something he could use in place of a rolling pin. "Where's this document I'm supposed to sign?"

"Forget that. You've not been yourself," Anthony said. "There's been talk around the gym."

Duncan paused from where he was washing the outside of a water bottle and frowned at his friend. Was this some sort of intervention? "What are people saying?"

"That you're acting more like me."

"How?"

"You haven't said more than two sentences outside of a class all week," Anthony said.

Notching his chin upward, Duncan said, "I didn't know introversion was a crime. But I'll tell you what, I'll smile a little more for you if that will make you feel better—"

"See," Anthony said, pointing at him. "Twins."

Duncan sighed, returning to the baking task in front of him. He pushed the water bottle over the dough, watching it flatten before his eyes. "I'll be back to normal once I get through the divorce party."

"That's what inspired this?" Anthony asked, gesturing to his flour stained torso and cluttered counter.

Using the open side of a glass, Duncan cut out the dough. "Yup."

"What about Retta?"

The bell went off telling him the oven had finished preheating.

"What about her?"

"You haven't talked about what happened at the wedding," Anthony said.

"The wedding was called off. But my job was done," he said, focusing on placing the dough on the tray without ripping it.

Duncan had fully expected to run into Retta while

taking out the garbage or arriving at work for the day. He'd even planned how he'd react and what he'd say. But in the weeks since the wedding, he hadn't seen so much as her apron strings.

"Did you want it to be done?" Anthony asked.

"What kind of question is that? It was a fake relationship." He tossed the tray into the oven. "Of course I wanted it to be done."

"So, you've started seeing other people?"

Duncan shrugged. "I've been talking." He'd only downloaded the app. "But of course business has been busy, so not a lot of time to go out."

"Hm. You're not too busy to bake really bad pastries though," Anthony said.

"This is therapeutic, believe it or not. You should appreciate that since you've suddenly turned into a counselor," Duncan said, discarding the dirty bowls and tools in the sink.

They sat in silence for a few minutes, watching a scene from a popular show play out on his TV screen.

"Also, if my memory serves me correctly, you were against this at the beginning. Why do you care?" Duncan asked.

"I know I'm probably the last person you should take relationship advice from, considering I'm hung up on…" Anthony straightened and cleared his throat.

Frowning, Duncan studied his friend. For the years they'd known each other, Anthony hadn't been in any standout relationships.

"You're interested in someone?" Duncan asked.

"No, n-never mind that," Anthony said. "My point is there's only room for one grumpy person, so maybe you should reevaluate this breakup with Retta."

To what end? He liked her, but it wasn't as if he was in

love with her. Plus, they'd already exceeded the length of time he usually spent in a real relationship.

The oven timer went off, and Duncan pulled out the scones. He looked at the flat, misshapen product and laughed. "I view relationships like this. You can start with the best intentions—I woke up today wanting to make blueberry scones. I followed all the rules from the expert"— Duncan shook the paper the recipe was written on—"and it still ended up like this."

He pointed at the tray of unsalvageable mess.

"Maybe she's worth the attempt," Anthony said, standing up and heading to the door. "And the reason your scones are fucked is because you used rice flour."

Duncan picked up the bag and read the label then swore under his breath.

Before Anthony closed the door behind himself, he said, "The good thing is, next time you'll know better."

———

When Retta returned home from the wedding weekend from hell, she wasn't surprised to see the world had continued to turn despite the fact she was simultaneously restless and numb.

That being said, she refused to continue to wallow. This was a "breakup" with a guy she'd grown fond of during the span of a few months, not a boyfriend of many years. That's why she'd wasted no time in setting up another date with Steve.

"I can't believe we finally got around to having a second one of these," Steve said, pushing his auburn hair from his face to look at her.

It was a little before noon on a Sunday, and they strolled through a park near her apartment. Joggers and cyclists passed them, while families set up for picnics on the grass on either side of the path they walked on.

"Me neither," Retta replied, making an effort to smile and look him in the eye every chance she got. She was determined to give him her full attention. No random thoughts about Duncan would prevail today.

"We've been having great weather so far this summer," Steve said as he turned his face upward, presumably to get the full effect of the sun.

"Yeah, but I think they're worried about wild fires up north because of the heat and the lack of rain."

"Oh, yeah. I think I heard something about that."

Struggling for a direction for their conversation, Retta tried to remember details from their first date they could discuss. What had drawn her to him? Why had she been hurt when he hadn't texted back? She remembered what he was wearing, but that was because he'd been in something similar to Duncan. And she wasn't supposed to be thinking about him.

The silence had gone on for too long, so Retta regrettably asked Steve about work. "Been to any more conferences lately?" The last thing she wanted to hear about was accounting.

"No, not since the last one you saw me at," he said, placing his hands into the pockets of his khakis.

She nodded but a follow-up question didn't come to mind.

"Pretty flowers," Steve said, pointing to the well-kept banks.

"I love the daisies."

Steve pretended as if he was writing down that statement in an invisible notebook. She laughed but immediately felt weird imagining him delivering her a bouquet.

Before her mind could insert a specific man she'd like

to receive daisies from, she nodded toward an ice cream cart ahead. "Do you want to grab something?"

"Funny," Steve replied.

Retta frowned, slowing her pace. "Why?"

"Lactose intolerant," he said.

Right.

"Yes, of course. I'm sorry," Retta said. They'd had a fifteen-minute conversation on their first date about dairy alternatives.

Long after they'd passed the ice cream cart, they still hadn't landed on a conversation topic of substance. Maybe they'd used up all their interesting stories during date number one.

When they moved out of the way of an approaching cyclist, Steve grabbed her arm to prevent her from falling into the large garden bed. As they straightened, she looked at the place where he'd been holding her. She felt nothing. It wouldn't be so notable if she couldn't imagine the sparks that would run across her body if—

God. When would these incessant thoughts end?

"I need to tell you something," Steve said when they stopped to watch some geese swim in the pond.

Was he not feeling it either? That would be the best-case scenario. They could go their separate ways without any hard feelings, and Retta wouldn't feel like this bad date was her fault.

"I googled you," Steve said, picking up a pebble from the ground and skipping it across the water.

Not what she expected.

"I've been trying to figure out a way to tell you, but I was worried you might think it was creepy—"

"Oh. Steve, don't worry about it. It's not a big deal."

He said something else after that, but she didn't hear it

because dread was setting in. She'd have to find a way to let him down easy after all.

"You're not enjoying yourself," Steve said, his statement cutting through all the mental noise.

She almost protested, but he'd handed her a perfect segue. "It's not you."

A cliché. Brilliant.

Steve smiled. "I suspected this might happen."

Retta straightened and looked directly at him. "Why?"

"When we bumped into each other at the conference, you told me you were seeing someone, and you looked really happy... You also called me 'Duncan' when we got out of our cars today."

Retta closed her eyes. "No, I didn't."

"It's fine."

"I'm so sorry. I-it's complicated."

Steve only reacted with a slight head tilt. "How complicated?"

"I think I'm in love with him," she said before letting out a big puff of air.

When the hell did that happen?

Steve nodded for an extended amount of time before saying, "Oh, okay. Cool."

She thought she had this under control, but her subconscious had decided to shove the truth to the forefront. Now she was back where she was a year ago: in love with someone who wasn't in love with her.

"We can talk about it," Steve said.

Retta massaged her temples. "Why would you want to hear all that?"

"Both my parents are therapists. I grew up talking everything out. It helps. Also, it's clear I have no chance."

She was about to reject the offer and simply wait till

she saw her friends to unload, but she was still buzzing from her admission. "Fine. Sure. We can do that."

They found a vacant bench facing the pond where Retta told Steve everything. Halfway through her retelling, she thought she might regret sharing so much. But Steve seemed actively engaged and unbothered by her rapid speech and expressive hands.

"Have you told him any of this?" Steve asked once she'd finished.

"No. Of course not. I know what he'd say."

There'd been a moment in her Grandmother's house when Duncan was about to leave, where she could have expressed her feelings as rudimentary and unclear as they were at the time. But she already knew what his response would be, so she saved both of them the humiliation.

"No. You *think* you know what he'd say," Steve said.

She frowned at his words.

"What if he surprises you? What if he has had a change of heart?"

Retta's head tipped backward. "You sound like my best friend."

Perking up, Steve asked, "Is she single and not in love with someone else?"

"No," Retta said as she laughed for the first time that day. "She has a man and a whole baby on the way."

Shrugging, Steve said, "I tried. But in all seriousness, let's say you tell Duncan your feelings and he rejects you. At least you know for sure. There's no guessing, and more importantly, there's no regret."

"But it'll hurt," she said.

"And you'll recover."

Retta didn't say anything for a moment. She'd run away from her emotions for so long but doing so never truly made her feel better. Sometimes it even made her feel worse and do weird things like take a fake boyfriend to her ex's wedding. Maybe it was time for a new strategy.

Looking up at Steve, Retta said, "If you're this good with the advice, I might have to book an appointment with one of your parents."

———

"I'm waiting for this to get less weird," Gwen said as she approached and handed Duncan a drink.

His parent's divorce party was being held in a private room inside a generic restaurant, and the overall mood was light. They remained glued to each other's sides, laughed with guests, and kissed the other as if they were in attendance for an entirely different celebration.

"Yeah, I don't think that's going to happen," he said.

"On the bright side, they look happy," Gwen said.

Duncan sighed and looked at his sister. "There's still time for them to fight about something."

Gwen nodded. "Of course, I said they looked happy. I didn't say they miraculously turned into different people."

As the two siblings stood there watching the scene in front of them unfold, Gwen's boyfriend, Eric, joined them.

"Hey, man, long time no see," Eric said as the two men embraced.

"Yeah, welcome back," Duncan replied. "How was the trip?"

"Good. Really good. Montreal is gorgeous. It made the job offer look even more appealing," Eric said, taking a bite from his vegetarian hors d'oeuvre.

This was the first time he was hearing about this. Duncan expected there'd be an engagement in the future for the two, but he'd never thought he'd live in a different city than his sister. That would be an adjustment.

"You got a job offer?" Gwen asked, frowning. "You didn't tell me that."

"We'll talk about it," Eric replied.

The couple seemed to silently communicate several more points before Gwen turned to him and asked, "How's Retta? I'm thinking of getting some baked goods for my class for the start of the school year."

Duncan winced.

"Oh, God, don't tell me you've broken up already," Gwen said.

"We were never really together."

"Okay, fine, but you liked her," Gwen said before turning to her boyfriend. "You should've seen him the first time I met her. He spotted her, and it was as if I was no longer there."

Eric raised his brows. "Then what's the problem, man?"

"There's no problem," Duncan replied. In fact, he was doing well. His mood wasn't as sour, and he had plans to go out next weekend to a bar for the first time in months.

Before they could engage in a back and forth, a delicate tinkling sound drew their attention to the front of the room. It was time for speeches. In all honesty, Duncan had done his best not to think about this function too much. And as a result, today would be the first time he looked at his speech since he proofread it several weeks ago.

One by one, people got up to stand behind the podium and tell stories about Trudy and Malcolm's lives together. A lot of those stories made their marriage sound like a quirky sitcom where the main couple simply bickered about empty milk cartons in the fridge.

"They look great together," Duncan's aunt, his mother's sister, said during her speech. "I think they stayed married this long because they were scared they wouldn't find better-looking people than each other. I can't blame them. It's rough out here."

Each speaker would end their spiel by raising a toast to an amicable separation and continued happiness. And when his sister was up, it was no different. She delivered a speech that was absolutely beautiful but wholly skimmed over the mess in their childhood.

By the time it was Duncan's turn, he was mildly irritated. He walked to the front of the room, looking out to the dining area that held forty people who'd played some role in his life in the past twenty-nine years. Duncan studied his cue cards and said, "Good afternoon, distinguished guests... and Uncle Peter."

There was laughter as everyone turned to the man who'd shown up to the event in jeans and a Toronto Maple Leafs cap.

"I thought this was a casual thing!" he shouted good-naturedly.

Duncan looked down at his notes where his next points were perfectly laid out. He was supposed to share a story about how his family missed their flights one summer because his parents couldn't stop arguing long enough to get them to the airport on time.

But the combination of the previous sanitized speeches and thoughts that had been ruminating since Anthony's pseudo-intervention, made him pause. Duncan was so opposed to risk, to conflict. It had been in the very fabric of his childhood and that made it especially tiresome.

He looked back up to the audience, who must've thought he'd suffered some sort of stroke because they were looking at him with furrowed brows.

Discarding the cue cards on the podium, Duncan

pulled out his phone where he'd typed out the vent speech Retta had suggested he write. He'd written this alternative reflection a week or so after he'd returned from the wedding. There'd been a night when he had trouble falling asleep. Instead of scrolling through social media, he'd opened up his notes app and let the words flow.

He knew the whole point was not to read it out loud, but it wasn't like he cussed out his parents in it, so what the hell.

"We're gathered here today to celebrate the demise of my parent's marriage," Duncan said. "At first, I was annoyed that this celebration was even happening, but if we can't celebrate these two agreeing on something, what can we celebrate?"

People in the room laughed.

"My parents loved my sister and me. Still do from what I've been told, but I won't lie and say growing up with them in the house was easy."

The mood in the room shifted with his last sentence.

Looking up he said, "I won't go into detail because that's probably best done with a therapist. Which, while I speak, I'm realizing I should probably get one."

He took a breath and read once again from the screen. "You both taught me a lot. Mom, you never believed in gender roles, and I credit you for me being self-sufficient."

He'd been around too many grown men who didn't know how to cook or only changed their bedsheets twice a year to take that aspect of his rearing for granted.

"Dad, you're curious and humble. I'd ask you the most inane questions and instead of brushing me off or pretending like you knew the answer, you'd tell me you didn't know. I'd forget I even asked the question, and two days later, you'd come to me with an essay with all the information you'd found. I thought it was the teacher in you, but now I think you just gave a shi—crap."

Duncan stopped. He wasn't really sure where he was heading with this runaway speech, this was never meant to be cohesive. But nobody had thrown tomatoes at him yet, and his sister wasn't giving him a signal to shut up, so he continued.

"But I think the biggest thing you taught me is I don't want a love like yours."

Again, he looked at his sister to gauge how far he was going. Though she looked melancholic, there was no indication that he needed to quit while he was ahead.

"I thought love only equaled strife, like it was supposed to be hard and filled with angst, and I've run away too often from anything close to that. Which I think can be a good thing because you avoid horrible relationships. But you also give up early because you anticipate the bad…"

Duncan looked up at his audience. "Even when the woman is the most creative, vibrant person you know. You end up pushing her away or not saying something because you're scared that it'll end badly. But how is that fair to her or me, for that matter?"

Stepping away from the podium without his notes, he said, "Like how can someone who makes you feel so happy simply by being in their presence be wrong for you? Maybe I haven't been reading the recipe correctly. Maybe I've been using rice flour instead of the regular kind, and I gave up without giving it a second look…"

The narrative thread had been lost.

Duncan clenched and unclenched his jaw before raising his empty hand like he held a glass. "To Trudy and Malcolm Gilmore."

He walked back to his seat on wooden legs and sat down as the next person spoke.

"Can," his sister whispered to him from the side of her mouth. "I expect a friend and family discount at a certain bakery soon?"

He looked at Gwen, his heartbeat refused to settle, and he wasn't sure if he said anything. But in his head, he heard a resounding, "yes."

Chapter Twenty

RETTA HAD BEEN PLANNING what she'd say to Duncan all weekend. However, when she thought of something, his possible rejection would immediately follow. She wanted to be succinct but not leave words unsaid. And clarity was of the utmost importance.

On the day she was making her profession, she'd taken to roughly handling dough and blasting pop music through the kitchen to distract herself from the knowledge that he was a few meters away. You can't slip into pining and stressing when someone is singing in falsetto over a synth.

Even when the day officially ended, she had to sit tight another hour as the technician she'd been waiting months for, fixed the water heater. The man was talkative and went on about the new uniforms the company had bought them. It distracted her for a bit. However, by the time he completed his task and handed her the invoice, she was about ready to jump out of her skin.

"Thank you so much," Retta said as she quickly guided the man to the door. "I really appreciate it."

"Yeah, it's a common problem," he said, halting before

they reached the exit. "You know, one time I was called out to a swanky little neighborhood. The houses over there are so big that my clients didn't hear all the rattling, and their basement ended up flooding."

"Oh, wow. That's unfortunate," she said, as she swung the door wide open. "You have a great evening now."

Once alone in the bakery, Retta made sure her face looked as good as it could after a thirteen-hour workday and slung several canvas bags and her purse across her body. The weight of her belongings on her literal shoulders was the only thing that made her feel like she wasn't going to float up and wither. Her stomach was in knots, and she wished she hadn't eaten so many ginger cookies in the past hour.

While doing her final scan of the store, she spotted a screwdriver the technician must've left. She'd decided to call about the forgotten item the next day when a knock sounded from the front. Expecting to find the man who'd left her store not even ten minutes ago, Retta opened the door with a smile and the tool in hand. But her expression dropped into a frown when she saw who stood there instead.

"I come in peace," Chris said as he raised his hands and studied the screwdriver she wielded.

Retta dropped her arm. "What are you doing here?"

Her ex-boyfriend was the last person she expected to see today.

"I was in the neighborhood, and I saw the lights were on," he said.

So, he decided to swing by to say hello?

"Can we talk?" he asked after several seconds of silence.

This was probably a bad idea, but she walked back into the bakery and gestured for him to follow.

After removing two upturned chairs from the table and taking a seat, Retta asked, "How are you doing?"

He rubbed his palms against his thighs. "I'm okay."

His beard looked dry and misshapen, his clothes were wrinkled, and his eyes had bags underneath them.

The last update Retta heard about her cousin was that she was in Portugal, but there was no way that Chris didn't know that. So, he wasn't here for an update on his ex-fiancée's whereabouts.

"Why are you here, Chris?"

He took a breath and said, "From what I understand you were the last person to speak to Irene before…"

"Yeah, I was," she said.

They sat in silence until he asked, "Can you give me an idea what she said to you? About me."

Retta swallowed hard. She didn't want to betray her cousin's confidence. If she had something to say to Chris, she would reach out. "I can't do that."

He nodded, but his eyes welled.

Oh, crap. This was the first time she was seeing him cry. He always seemed too in control and self-important to display such emotions.

She shoved her hand in one of the bags she was still wearing, searching for tissue.

"Chris, I'm sorry—"

Her words were cut off by a choppy sob he let out.

"I-is. This. How. You. Felt. When. We. Broke. Up?" he asked loudly as tears soaked his chin.

There was a part of her that wanted to balk at his question. She didn't spend close to a year acting like everything was peachy just to admit to him she'd been angry and hurt over their breakup, but he was clearly distraught. Whatever modicum of pride she'd tried to maintain through cool indifference didn't matter anymore. The man was open-mouth crying in front of her.

"Kind of," she said, handing him a napkin. "It didn't really come at the best time for me. And you dating my cousin after didn't help."

After wiping his tears and blowing his nose, Chris sat there staring off into the distance.

This could be her in a few hours on her best friend's couch once she talked to Duncan, but then she'd figure out how to move on just like she'd moved on from Chris.

"Can I give you some advice?" Retta asked.

He didn't respond, but he looked at her, waiting.

"I would give her time. I don't know if she wants anything to do with you, but the worst thing you could do right now is try to pursue her," Retta said.

Chris nodded, taking a shuddering breath before standing up and walking to the door. She followed behind with growing buoyancy in her body.

"Thanks for speaking to me," he said, once he took a step outside. "I know with our past you didn't have to."

Retta nodded. "Have a good evening. And good luck."

The resounding ring of the bell as she closed the door made her feel like she'd finally shut that chapter in her life. Now for the new one.

———

It was close to the end of the workday for Duncan when he went outside to change the sidewalk signage. As it was customary, he looked over to the front area of the Dutch Oven. He didn't know what he expected to find there other than cold concrete. It had only been a few days since the divorce party, but he'd contemplated long and hard about how he'd approach Retta.

His impulse was to walk over to her store or show up at her apartment and tell her what he was feeling. But if he was going to give this relationship thing a go, he had to do it right. Romance was the name of the game.

He thought of doing something with Post-it notes or sending her tickets to the drive-in theatre screening *Rocky* next month. With all the options and what was at stake, Duncan had become nervous he'd blow his chance. However, he'd given himself till the end of the week to make a move.

As he stood back to look at his altered sign, the door to Retta's bakeshop opened. She should've been home at this time. Dammit. He could quickly step inside the gym and avoid her, especially since he hadn't been to his barber in weeks, but he didn't want to. It had been too long since he'd seen her.

Pushing back his shoulders, he waited for her to exit. However, when someone stepped out, it was Christopher. Duncan stopped breathing. Her ex was technically single now, but she wouldn't get back with him. Would she? Retta's profile was only visible for a few seconds before she closed the door.

Maybe she wasn't over him, and this profession that he'd been constructing in his head was not going to be well received. The thought made his stomach roll. Wouldn't that be some sick joke to have the woman he wanted to seriously be with for the first time not want him back?

As Christopher passed him on the way to the parking lot, he looked Duncan in the eye and nodded. Was that smugness? Had he made a formal request for her to forget how he'd broken her heart? Before Duncan could talk himself out of it, he was eliminating the distance between him and the front of her store. The door swung open almost immediately after he'd knocked.

"Wh—" Retta's eyes widened.

God, how he'd missed gazing into those eyes that looked like churning vats of dark chocolate.

"Hi," she said as she adjusted one of the several bags strapped to her body. "Come in."

Good sign. She was receptive to talking to him.

"How are you?" he asked.

She studied him for a moment before saying, "My day just turned around."

Fuck.

He stuffed his hands in his pockets and attempted to gather his thoughts. "T-that's good."

"Yeah, I've been meaning to—"

A cell phone rang from the depths of one of Retta's bags. She smiled as she waited for it to go to voicemail.

"Sorry," she said, clearing her throat. "Actually, do you want anything? Water, coffee, orange juice?"

"No, I'm good."

"Okay, great. Um. What I was saying before was, these last few—"

The ringing started up again.

Retta smiled through a wince. "Give me a second." She shoved her hand into her purse and rummaged through it.

"We can talk later," he said over the phone's noise.

Now that he was thinking clearly again, he knew he couldn't do this off the cuff. If he was competing with another man, he had one shot to make her believe that he was the better choice.

"No," she said, her voice echoing in the empty bakery. "I mean if you don't have to be somewhere right now, I'd like for you to stay."

She dropped her bags on the floor and got low to search them.

"Hello?" Retta said as she finally found her phone and answered it. "Wait, right now?"

Her suddenly shrill voice made Duncan freeze where he stood and study her.

"Oh, God. Okay, I'm coming. Just remember to breathe." Once she hung up, she looked at him and said, "I have to go."

"Retta, is everything okay?"

She spun in circles. "Where are my keys? Where are my keys?"

He spotted them on the ground nearby and picked them up for her.

"Thank you," she said as she retrieved her belongings from the floor. "My friend's in labor. Her partner is stuck in traffic on the other side of town, and I just need to get to her."

"Let me help you," he said, reaching for her bags.

They left the bakery together and jogged to where she'd parked her vehicle. However, looking up and down the length of the street, he couldn't spot her tiny gray car. She pressed the alarm on her keys several times but there was no responding siren.

"Oh my God," she whispered as her chin trembled. "It finally happened. They towed my car."

"Everything's going to be okay," Duncan said, already on the move toward the gym. "Head over to my truck. I'm gonna grab my keys."

———

Duncan returned before Retta had a chance to do more than pace and open up the notes on her phone from the one birthing class she'd attended with Kym.

"It's going to be okay," he said again as he backed out

of the parking lot and followed her directions to Kym's house.

He said it so confidently that she chose to believe him. They arrived at their destination in less than ten minutes.

Charging through the front door Kym had left unlocked, Retta shouted her friend's name. She found her doubled over her dining room table, groaning into the crook of her arm.

"Oh, thank God," Kym said as she looked up. "I thought I'd have to *Little House on the Prairie* this shit."

Retta tried to hide her panic at seeing the puddle underneath her friend's feet. Instead, she approached and helped her straighten. "Okay, let's go have this baby."

"My hospital bag is in the coat closet," Kym said as she pushed her braids over her shoulder and attempted to catch her breath.

"I'll grab it when we pass by," Retta said, as she gently walked her friend forward. Unfortunately, at this pace, the baby would be teething by the time they arrived at the hospital. "Honey, I need you to move a little quicker."

"I"—Kym breathed hard and doubled over—"can't."

"I can help," Duncan said, stepping forward.

Both women looked up. Retta had forgotten he was there, but he was holding Kym's beige hospital bag and looked like he could move a mountain if he really wanted to. An unexpected calmness settled over her.

"Who the hell are you?" Kym asked, sweat coming down her face.

"This is Duncan."

"Oh. You guys back together? For real?" Kym asked as she reached for him.

He immediately drew closer and scooped her into his arms. They both ignored the question but briefly shared a glance. That was yet to be determined. But now wasn't the time to think about all of that.

Once Kym was seated in the backseat, she said, "So, Duncan, I wish we were meeting when I'm not in pain and dilating, but it's good to put a face to a name."

Retta tensed. She didn't need her friend revealing too much about her feelings for Duncan before she had the chance to do it.

Kym temporarily abandoned the topic when another contraction hit.

"Remember the breathing," Retta said, twisting to look at her and perform the quick, sharp breaths with her.

After the cramps subsided, her friend said, "You know, I told Retta that I thought the whole fake relationship thing was ridiculous, not to mention attending her ex's wedding. But everything worked—"

Kym groaned and Retta wanted to join her. She hadn't told Duncan anything about Chris. He probably thought her even more pathetic for attending the wedding. But when she braved a glance at him, he didn't look remotely shocked at the information.

"You know," she said.

Duncan looked at her. "Know what?"

"That Chris is my ex."

"Yeah, I found out at the engagement party."

Shaking her head, she said, "Why didn't you say anything?"

He shrugged. "We had an agreement for me to attend a wedding. It didn't matter whose it was."

"Oh, fuck," Kym said before she let out an extended groan that turned into a scream.

"We're almost there," Duncan said as he turned onto the street the hospital was on.

When they finally arrived at the emergency room, Len was already there, and medical professionals took over.

Len and Retta surrounded Kym as she pushed and yelled.

"I can see the head," a nurse said after some time.

Retta wiped her friend's brow. "You're so close."

Kym tightened her already death grip on Retta's hand, but dammit, at this point, if her friend wanted to throw her against the wall, she would let her.

Thankfully, none of that was necessary because a baby was born minutes later, wailing and healthy.

———

Duncan stood up the moment Kym's partner emerged from the back of the emergency room still donning his hair cover. They'd briefly seen each other as the nurses had rolled Kym to the back. From the way the man was smiling and practically skipping toward Duncan, he knew it was good news.

Regardless, he asked, "How's everything?"

"It's a boy," the new father said loudly.

A few people in the waiting room whooped and clapped.

"And he's good?" Duncan asked. "Kym?"

"They're both doing well," he said, barely containing his giddiness. "Thank you so much for getting them here."

He then moved in for a hug that Duncan accepted.

"There's no need to thank me. I'm glad I was there at the right time."

When they separated the man said, "I should let you go and enjoy the rest of your evening."

Duncan briefly looked past the father's shoulder. "Oh, I thought I'd wait for Retta and drop her off."

"Don't worry about that. I'll drive her home."

Nodding, Duncan ignored the burning in his chest and said, "Congratulations and all the best."

When he strode out of the hospital, he found the sun setting but the air still warm. This was for the best. He'd head back to the gym and make sure closing went smoothly, and he'd spend the rest of the evening figuring out what he'd say to Retta. A few paces from his car, someone called his name from behind. Turning around, he found Retta running toward him, her black dress billowing around her.

"You okay?" he asked, jogging to meet her halfway.

"I'm fine," she said, breathing heavily and smoothing down her hair. "I'm a godmother." Her beautiful smile lit up her entire face.

His hands ached to touch her. "You're going to be amazing."

They stood there for a moment, listening to the traffic and ambulance sirens around them. Maybe this was the chance he was supposed to take. Forget grand gestures and possible rejection. He had to make his feelings known even if they weren't clearly mapped out in his head.

"We didn't finish our conversation back at the bakery."

"I need to tell you something."

They said simultaneously.

Her eyebrows came together as she pushed her glasses up her face. "What?"

Rubbing the back of his neck, he said, "When we made our agreement, parking spots were all I wanted. But somewhere along the way, maybe between a carnival ride and an engagement party, that changed."

Retta's mouth fell open on a small gasp.

His heart raced, but he stepped closer. "I've been terri-fied to see what that change means, but I don't want to pull my punches anymore. And I know you have feelings for Christopher but—"

She shook her head so furiously that he stopped talking.

Before he could interpret her response differently, she grabbed his face and said, "I don't have feelings for Chris."

Duncan could now feel his heartbeat in his throat as he let her words register. "No?"

She shook her head again and opened her mouth to say something, but he descended on her lips before she had the chance to. The tension in his body was replaced with the heat of their kiss and the gentleness of her hands that still held his face. She tasted of sugar and ginger, and he poured every ounce of longing from the past weeks into his caresses. He broke their kiss to look into her eyes.

"What does this mean?" she whispered.

He gently brushed some hair from her face and said, "It means I want to do this relationship thing with you. For real this time. I love you too fucking much to not give us a shot."

Retta closed her eyes as a smile grew on her face. "I've been wanting to tell you the same thing all day."

Tightening his hands where they held her waist, he asked, "What? What did you want to tell me?" He needed to hear her say it.

"That I love you," she said, wrapping her arms around his neck. "And I want to do this relationship thing with you too."

He let out a long breath as lightheadedness swept through him. After he regained some semblance of control, he leaned his forehead against hers and said, "Good. I wasn't a big fan of my girl being in love with someone else."

"Your girl? It's day one," she said, laughing lightly.

"Nah, day one started the moment you thought I was your date at that coffee shop."

"You're right," she said, detaching from him and moving toward his truck. "And as my official, very real boyfriend you should know I'll need one to two of your hoodies, your Netflix login information, and a ride until I get my car back. Oh, and food."

Duncan grinned as he watched her saunter away. He'd give her that and whatever was humanly possible.

Grabbing her hand, he spun her back to him. "Deal. And you're in luck, I happen to have a really good scone recipe at home."

The End

THANK YOU

Thank you so much for reading *Make a Scene*. I hope you enjoyed getting to know Retta and Duncan. I'll be back soon with Gwen and Anthony's story! You can visit www. mimigracebooks.com and sign up for my newsletter to receive updates. Again, thanks for reading. Your support means the world.

Mimi <3

ABOUT THE AUTHOR

Mimi Grace credits romance novels for turning her into a bookworm at twelve years old. It didn't matter if those stories included carriages or cowboys, she could be found past her bedtime getting lost in a couple's journey to happily-ever-after.

Today, she writes fun, sexy books that she calls confetti and spice for your bookshelf.

Besides romance novels, she loves generous servings of mint chocolate chip ice cream, long-running reality competition shows, and when she correctly spells "necessary".

instagram.com/mimigracebooks

twitter.com/mimigracebooks

facebook.com/mimigracebooks

CPSIA information can be obtained
at www.ICGtesting.com
Printed in the USA
LVHW030119170821
695429LV00005B/176

9 781999 108236